Beyond
Providence

Beyond Providence

STEVEN SCHNUR

HARCOURT BRACE & COMPANY

San Diego   New York   London

Copyright © 1996 by Steven Schnur

Requests for permission to make copies of any part
of the work should be mailed to: Permissions Department,
Harcourt Brace & Company, 6277 Sea Harbor Drive,
Orlando, Florida 32887-6777.

Library of Congress Cataloging-in-Publication Data
Schnur, Steven.
Beyond Providence/Steven Schnur.—1st ed.
p. cm.
Summary: Twelve-year-old Nathan comes of age on a beloved yet
dilapidated farm as he struggles to understand the death of his
mother amidst the anger and violence of his father and brother.
ISBN 0-15-200982-5   ISBN 0-15-200981-7 (pbk.)
[1. Fathers and sons—Fiction.   2. Farm life—Fiction.
3. Death—Fiction.]   I. Title.
PZ7.S3644Be   1996
[Fic]—dc20   95-30929

Text was set in Granjon
Designed by Lori J. McThomas
First edition
A B C D E
A B C D E (pbk.)
Printed in Hong Kong

For my beloved nieces and nephews,
Jessica, Donna, Madeleine, Sam, Max

Part One

"Two lambs were born last night," Pa said as I came down to breakfast. Hunter stirred beside the stove, opened one eye, wagged his tail, then fell back asleep. A thin column of steam rose from the kettle, fogging the kitchen window. Outside, the snow blew hard, rattling the shutters.

"They gonna be warm enough?" I asked, thawing my frozen fingers on the cup of cocoa Pa handed me. The floor was ice-cold. I sat at the kitchen table and drew my bare feet under me.

"It's not the cold I'm worried about. Where're your socks?"

"Kitty's darning 'em."

"Well, go get them on," he said, zipping up his padded blue coveralls and pulling on boots. "Milk before haying. The lambs'll need the bottle. Ewe's gone dry."

His eyes avoided mine as he pulled on his stiff leather gloves. Mama would have known where the bottle was. Milking the goats and nursing the newborn lambs had always been her job. Now it was up to Kitty and me.

"Do you know where it is?" I asked softly.

"What?"

"The bottle?"

"Here someplace. Where's Kitty? It's late. Snow's no reason to go slack. We're behind enough as it is." He paused with his hand on the door. "And you tell Eric I want that harness mended by noon."

"He's still asleep."

"Well, get him up," he snapped, opening the back door. A swirl of snow salted the air, scattering papers on his desk. Pa stepped out into the storm and yanked the door shut, shaking the wall.

Through the kitchen window I watched him lean forward into the wind, limping badly. Damp, cold mornings were hardest on his leg. Whenever it slowed him down, he slapped his right thigh in frustration, muttering, "Come on now!" just as he did to the horses when they grew contrary.

Twice the wind nearly knocked him off his feet, sending him hopping backward, arms outstretched, and then near the barn he went down, disappearing in a waist-high drift. Just as quickly he hopped back onto his good leg, his right hand pressed hard against his hip.

As he swung open the barn door, a puff of white smoke blew out into the storm, circled twice, and returned inside.

"Morning, Bianca," I murmured. Ever since

Mama left, the white dove had perched among the rafters, her solitary cooing sounding like the barn's own heartbeat.

Kitty joined me in the kitchen, kissing the top of my head. "Where are your socks, young man?" she burst out. "It must be ten degrees outside!"

"Six," I corrected.

"You ninny. You'll catch your death."

"You were fixing 'em."

She rummaged through her apron pockets. "You take care of these," she said, handing them to me.

As I pulled them on, she poured herself a cup of coffee and stared out at the storm. Her springy red hair lay coiled on her head, dozens of strands escaping in all directions like tiny flames. Kitty was forever tucking them back in place and smoothing her skirt and blouse. She refused to "dress for the dirt," as she put it, insisting that one could live just as cleanly on a farm as she had in town before moving in with us. Pa told her she was wasting her time scouring floors that turned muddy the moment we walked through the door. "That's why God created the doormat," she told him. Kitty was determined to change our ways; Pa was equally intent on living just the way he had when Mama was alive, indifferent to dirt.

"Two lambs were born last night," I told her, searching the kitchen shelves. "Pa needs the baby bottle."

"The lambs need it more," she said, cracking eggs into the skillet. "How's the ewe?"

"She's got no milk. Where do you think Mama left it?"

"You'd know better than I," she replied, her eyes searching mine. "Maybe Eric knows."

"He's not up yet."

Kitty laughed.

"How come he sleeps so much?" I asked.

"Because he's seventeen years old," she replied.

"Did you sleep that much when you were his age?"

"Don't make it sound like it was so long ago," she answered. "Boys are different."

"Will I be like him?"

"Nathan, you worry too much to sleep late. You're going to be the world's first twelve-year-old boy to run his own farm."

She lay long strips of bacon in a second pan, then stood back as the fat began to sizzle. Hunter rose stiffly, walked once around the kitchen in search of scraps, then returned to his bed.

"Something's going on up there," Kitty remarked, looking out at the barn. "Uncle Ray's never late for breakfast." She speared a piece of bacon with a long fork, let it cool a moment, then took a bite.

"Give him a holler," she said, removing the skillet from the fire.

I slid over to the door and stuck my face out

into the storm. "Breakfast, Pa!" I shouted. A blast of cold air sent sheets of snow against the house.

"Shut the door!" Kitty cried. We waited another minute. "You better go check," she suggested.

Reluctantly, I yanked my coat from the peg and pulled on boots.

"Don't be long," she said, covering the steaming plates, "or there'll be nothing left but crumbs."

I fought my way through the wind and high snow past Dart and Doc, who stood snorting in the lee of the barn. Small clouds of steam rose from their nostrils as they pulled at a fresh bale of hay, their high backs and wheat-colored manes bleached white with snow. The goats huddled in the lean-to, except Gretchen, who ambled toward me, her bag heavy with milk.

"I'll be right back," I said, patting her head through the fence.

"Pa, breakfast," I called, entering the barn. Bianca leapt from the cross beam and floated toward the sheep cote, her white feathers glowing in the darkness.

"Come here, son," Pa called. I found him kneeling in the straw among the sheep. The two newborn lambs, one white, the other black, lay bleating in a small fenced-off paddock, buried up to their noses in fresh straw. The rest of the flock stood huddled together by the corral door, all facing the same way. The cold air smelled of mutton, manure, and hay.

"She's not gonna make it," Pa said, nodding toward the ewe lying at his knees. Her bushy gray coat was matted with dried blood and straw. He smoothed the wool away from her exhausted eyes.

"What's wrong with her?"

"Bad birth. Two big lambs. Tore her up inside. Did you find the bottle?"

"Not yet." I shrank back, expecting his anger.

"Those lambs are hungry," he said.

"I'm still looking," I answered. "Kitty says breakfast's ready."

"Start without me."

"What are you gonna do?"

"Not much I can do." He carded the ewe's matted wool between bloodstained fingers. "Have to cull her. She was a good breeder."

"What about the lambs?" I asked, watching the black one struggle onto uncertain legs in the shifting straw.

"We'll try grafting them." Pa rose with difficulty.

"Couldn't we just bottle-feed 'em?"

"Runts them. It's okay for two or three days, till the milk comes in, after that it's nothing but trouble. You give one animal special care, the others suffer. Nature does its own culling. Go eat your breakfast, then get milking. Gretchen's near bursting."

The black lamb tried to squeeze through the paddock fence, bleating loudly as I turned to go. His mother lifted her head and gathered in her legs in an effort to stand, then collapsed back into the straw, her black eyes staring vacantly at Pa. I wanted to help her, but there was nothing I could do.

Bianca followed me out of the barn, her wings snapping as she struggled against the storm. She settled under the peak of the barn roof, her feathers rustling in the wind. "No hawks today," I called up to her. She cooed deep in her throat, then puffed out her white chest.

"Boots!" Kitty cried.

"Pa said to start without him. The ewe's dying." I kicked off my boots, then joined her at the table.

"Poor thing," she said, pursing her lips and shaking her head. "What will happen to the lambs?"

"Pa's gonna try and get one of the other ewes to nurse 'em."

A few minutes later he burst into the kitchen on a gust of icy wind.

"Morning, Uncle Ray," Kitty said.

"Morning," he replied, blowing on his bare, bloodstained hands. His face had the dark, concentrated look he wore when shearing and butchering.

"Your boots," she said.

"Hang my boots," he growled.

"I'll hang you first," she returned. "I'm not washing this floor twenty times a day just because you're too lazy to wipe your feet."

"Then don't," he snapped. "This is a farm, not a ballroom." He plodded over to the sink, melting snow dropping from him in a steady stream across the floor.

"Uncle Ray!" Kitty cried. "Just look at the mess you're making." She grabbed a dirty rag from beside the sink and began mopping up the puddles while Pa rolled up his sleeves and dunked his filthy hands in the dishwater.

"Not with the dishes!" Kitty screamed. "For God's sake, Uncle Ray!" She dropped her rag and hurriedly pulled plates and pans from the dirty water while he continued to scrub the blood and dirt from his fingers and forearms. Pa was a big man, thick about the waist and chest. Kitty was almost as broad. The two of them dwarfed the sink.

"You find that bottle yet?" he asked, splashing water over his face.

"Don't touch that dish towel," Kitty howled. Her hand shot out, but he reached it first, staining it gray.

"You *are* contrary this morning," she said, using a corner of the towel to wipe a spot of dried blood from his cheek.

"Leave me be," he complained, shaking his head.

"Eat your breakfast, Uncle Ray. You're nasty when you're hungry." She pulled his plate from the oven and poured him a fresh cup of coffee.

Pa ate quickly, frowning at his plate, hardly tasting his food. Ever since Mama died, some angry thought seemed to lie across his forehead, giving him a permanent scowl.

Overhead the ceiling creaked. Pa looked up, then muttered through a mouthful of eggs, "My brothers used to rip me from my bed if I wasn't up an hour before dawn."

"Beasts!" Kitty declared.

"We had a lot of mouths to feed."

"Well, there's a blizzard blowing out there today, for God's sake. What's the rush?"

"Animals need tending, snow or no snow. Goats are waiting," he reminded me.

"Bundle up," Kitty said as I stepped back into the storm.

CHAPTER

2

Pa and I had a silent understanding that one day I would take over the farm. It should have gone to Eric, as the oldest, and for a long time we both thought it would. By the time Eric was my age, he had learned to break horses, shear sheep, plow the fields, bring in the hay, and harvest the crops. He could repair harnesses, cultivators, and mowers as well as Pa, sometimes better. Eric had always been good with his hands and not only had more patience than Pa but wanted nothing so much as to please him. For Pa's fiftieth birthday he made Doc a new leather harness that was stronger and finer than anything in the town of Providence.

But around the time he turned fifteen, Eric began to lose interest in the farm, neglecting his chores, growing sullen. For as long as I could remember, he was always doodling, filling theme books with drawings. He could look at anything—a wildflower, a bird, a passing wagon—and draw it from memory days later. Mama said he had a natural talent and hung his pictures in the parlor. Pa said he didn't know about talent, but a man couldn't have two mistresses. It had to be one or the other, "and God knows that art of his won't fill his belly." Eric could scribble all he wanted, Pa said, so long as it didn't interfere with his chores.

But that's just what happened. Eric took to sleeping past breakfast, daydreaming through our morning lesson with Mama, then disappearing into the woods for hours. He and Pa began to argue almost every meal, and always over the same thing: Eric's forgotten or sloppy chores. Whenever Mama took Eric's side, saying things like, "It's his life," Pa shot back, "Not until he's twenty-one, it ain't. I haven't broken my back all these years to feed and clothe him just so he can run off the minute he's old enough to be some real help around here. This place doesn't farm itself."

One morning Pa took his belt to Eric for forgetting to hay the horses. He whipped him again three days later for coming home late, striking him across the face and leaving a large red welt that glared at us for weeks. With every fight, Mama got more upset, clasping her forearms nervously, begging them to stop. Eric just grew more defiant.

And then one evening the family came apart

forever. Pa had ordered Eric to plow the cornfield right after our morning lesson. But the afternoon passed without any sign of him. By supper, Pa was seething. When Eric strode through the door carrying a drawing pad and pencil, Pa blocked his path and snarled, "Where you been all this time?"

"Nowhere," Eric replied, avoiding his eyes.

"Didn't I tell you to get plowing after your lesson?" The muscles at the back of his jaw clenched and released as he waited for Eric's reply.

"Ray, leave him be, he's here now," Mama said, coming between them. She was a little woman, not half Pa's size. Even Eric towered over her. "Wash up, Eric, supper's getting cold."

Pa ignored her. "Answer me," he demanded.

"I had other things to do," Eric replied sullenly.

The slap was so hard that Eric dropped his pad.

"You had other things to do?" Pa raged. "When I say I want you plowing, you better be plowing."

Eric bent down for his pad, but Pa stepped on it.

"Ray, enough," Mama said, trying to push him back. Tears stood in Eric's eyes, but his mouth was just as defiant as Pa's.

"I'm sick and tired of his sass," Pa growled.

"And I'm sick and tired of you," Eric muttered.

Pa shoved Mama aside roughly and grabbed Eric by his upper arms, squeezing so tight the muscles on his forearms turned to stone.

"Ray, Eric, don't, please," Mama pleaded.

"You're sick and tired?" Pa raged, pinning Eric against the wall. I shrank into the shadows, afraid of getting caught between them.

"Let him go," Mama cried, trying to pry them apart.

"If I'd dared talk that way at his age, I'd have been beaten senseless and tossed out of the house," he declared. "You either earn your keep or get out."

"Ray!"

"I'm going," Eric said in a hoarse whisper.

"Go, get out!" Pa thundered, releasing him.

"I can't stand this anymore," Mama cried. She seemed to be coming apart inside.

Eric headed for the stairs.

"Where do you think you're going?" Pa snarled, grabbing his arm. "I said, get out!"

Eric shook loose of his grip. "I need my things."

"You have no things. I own the shirt on your back. Get out!"

"I'm not going to watch this any longer," Mama sobbed.

Neither of them heard her. Eric left the house

and vanished into the woods, then Pa stormed out to the barn.

The next morning Mama was gone. I thought at first she was up at the cabin. It was her favorite spot, perched on a rock ledge above the farm with a view of Providence and the blue hills beyond. The cabin had been abandoned years ago, the single empty room littered with leaves and broken glass and the droppings of wild animals. The surrounding woods teemed with wildflowers that Mama gathered in her apron and set in a vase on the kitchen table. A few gnarled apple trees still bore a bushel or two of cider apples. She always said the oldest trees bore the sweetest fruit.

When Eric was ten, she took us up to the cabin and told him that someday when he brought a wife back to the farm, Pa would help him fix up the place so he could have a house of his own. "You might even clear the land and plant it," she said. "This ridge needs more light."

But Eric lost interest in the cabin as he did the farm. Mama continued to cross the pasture and follow the narrow trail up to the ridge, watching the hawks circle or the sun set. When I joined her there one afternoon, she said in a dreamy, faraway voice that perhaps one day *I* would live there. I was proud to have taken Eric's place.

So when I came down to breakfast the morning after the last fight and found the supper dishes still on the table and the stove cold, I assumed Mama was up at the cabin. So did Pa. "Go fetch her," he snapped, setting to work on an empty stomach.

It was drizzling as I entered the woods. The trees wept cold, fat drops of rain. The cabin was empty. I peered in through a shattered window and whispered, "Mama." Something scurried for cover, leaving tiny tracks on the damp and dusty floor.

Overhead I heard a flutter of wings and a resonant cooing. Among the rafters perched a spotless white dove that strode nervously across the beam. When I stepped back from the window, she left her perch and flew to the sill, then fluttered into one of the ancient apple trees, watching me as I circled the cabin calling for Mama. After I gave up the search and headed back to the farm, she followed, darting from branch to branch. At the edge of the pasture she paused, afraid to fly out into the open. I walked on, looking back over my shoulder. She cooed loudly, leapt a few feet into the air, then doubled back for cover. I turned and held out my hand. To my surprise she glided on outstretched wings into my palm and remained there motionless, her tiny heart beating against my cupped hands. Near the barn she began to squirm. When I relaxed my grip she burst free with a powerful snap of her wings, sailed in through the open doors, and took shelter above the hayloft.

Morning and afternoon passed with no sign of

Mama. Eric, who had spent a wet night in the woods, slipped into the house while Pa was in the barn. He threw his clothes into a bag along with his paints and brushes and was about to leave for good when Pa came upon him in the kitchen, filling his pockets with food. Eric stiffened, so did I, but Pa just told us to hitch up the wagon. We were going looking for Mama. Eric seemed relieved.

Folks in Providence said they'd seen her walking toward the river six miles off, so we followed the road all the way to the pier but saw no sign of her.

Pa was stunned into muteness by Mama's disappearance. Eric tended to his chores. All fighting stopped. For weeks we ate nothing but cold mutton and eggs, wore the same filthy clothes day after day, and let the house grow rank and muddy.

Six weeks later a letter arrived bearing a New York City postmark. Pa threw it down unopened among the papers on his desk and went back out to the fields. He'd long since decided Mama had gone to the city, a trip she always wanted to make. Pa thought travel was a waste of time and money. I held the letter up to the window trying to read through the envelope. Eric finally grabbed it out of my hands and ripped it open.

"Pa's gonna be furious," I said.

"I don't care," he snapped, unfolding the letter.

I looked out the window a moment for Pa, then turned back. Eric was white.

"What's wrong?" I asked.

"Ma's dead," he whispered.

"What?"

"She drowned!" he muttered, handing me the letter.

It was from the captain of the *Holly Fair,* a side-wheeler that regularly made the overnight trip from Providence Township down the Hudson to New York City. There had been an accident the week before. As it left the pier for the trip upriver, the ship had collided with a barge, sinking in thirty feet of water. The captain had ordered all passengers into the lifeboats for the short trip to shore. No one had panicked. The evacuation, he wrote, "had proceeded without incident in a safe and orderly manner." But when the ship was raised several days later, they found Mama, "inexplicably" on the lowest deck, trapped near the engine room, the only passenger to drown in the accident. The city had buried her the following day.

I felt numb all over. Mama dead? She'd just gone away for a few weeks to rest. She'd be back. She'd never even said good-bye.

I took the letter and ran out to the cornfield where Pa was plowing.

"Pa!" I shouted. "Mama's drowned."

He just kept on walking behind Dart like he

didn't hear me. But I could tell from the set of his shoulders that he heard.

"Pa! Is it true?" Tears of frustration and terror filled my eyes.

When he got to the end of the row he called, "Go back to the house, son." I waited for him in the kitchen until dark, reading the letter over and over, hoping each time it would say something different.

Pa read it when he came in for dinner, then just stared across the table at the place where Mama usually sat. I put a plate of mutton in front of him. He ate a mouthful or two, then went to bed without saying a word. Eric and I didn't sleep much that night. I kept waking to find him standing at the window.

Pa drove himself harder than ever after that, rising earlier, working later, rarely speaking except to give orders. He never mentioned the accident or Mama. Eric and I did as we were told, feeling hollow and abandoned.

With no funeral to mark Mama's death, it was easy to imagine she hadn't really died, just disappeared. After the first shock wore off, I began to think maybe the letter was mistaken: Mama had never gotten on that steamship; a different Margaret Burns had died in the accident. For weeks I awoke each morning expecting her to walk through the door. Whenever a wagon or buggy drove up to the house, my heart leapt.

But spring turned to summer and then to fall with no change in the terrible silence surrounding us.

Once, unable to sleep, I asked Eric if he thought Mama was still alive. "Why should she have been the only one to drown?"

"Because she wanted to," he muttered from his bed.

"No, she didn't," I said, shocked by the idea.

"She wasn't coming back," he insisted. "She hated it here."

"Then what was she doing on the ship?" I asked, hot with anger and doubt.

"If it hadn't sunk she would have jumped overboard. I would, too, if I had to live here the rest of my life."

I wanted to hit him, but he was twice my size. "You're wrong," I insisted, my eyes filling with tears. "She'll come back. You'll see."

He grunted and rolled over, turning his back to me.

Then, just before harvest, Kitty, Pa's thirty-one-year-old niece, moved in with us, and for the first time in months we began to eat hot meals and wear clean clothes. Kitty understood Pa better than we did and never shied away from criticizing him. The arguments that turned bitter and violent in Mama's presence usually sputtered and died around Kitty. Yet, for all her kindness, Eric resented her, even when she defended him. But she understood that, too, and just let him be. To me she was half sister, half mother, and by the end of her first week with us I felt the empty, aching places of my soul begin to fill with a new love.

From the milking stand I looked across the white valley to the Hejdling farm, their neatly walled fields barely visible through the storm. We occupied most of the colder, eastern ridge just north of Providence, the Hejdlings all of the warmer western one with its early morning light and apple orchard shimmering in the late afternoon. Spring always came to their hillside first, the snow melting from their fields earlier than ours, their corn and wheat greening two weeks sooner. In autumn, the morning sun didn't melt the hoarfrost on our pastures until an hour or more after the Hejdlings' had shed their whiteness. In winter, their windows glowed not with the smoky oil lamps that sputtered in our house and barn but with the new electric lights just beginning to appear in Providence.

The Hejdlings had farmed their ridge since the Revolution, producing two or three boys and as many girls in every generation to help maintain their four hundred acres. The youngest child, Sonja, was eleven, a year younger than me; her sister, Lisa, was Eric's age. Gregory and Halvard had finished the village school years before and now helped run the farm. Bittle was two years older than me. Folks said he was simpleminded. His father and brothers didn't ask much of him around the farm. When he wasn't milking or doing odd chores, he was free to roam the woods. Mrs. Hejdling had died giving birth to Sonja.

Our two families had never been close. We were too busy managing our farm to devote much time to socializing, and Pa seemed to resent their success. When Eric turned sixteen, Mama had suggested he begin paying court to Lisa, believing that a marriage between the two families would ensure the future of our farm. But Eric and Lisa never got on. They were both headstrong and independent. I would have been happy with a smile from Sonja, but she ignored me, clinging to her golden-haired sister and adopting her haughty ways. Of the five Hejdling children, only Bittle showed me any kindness.

"I found it," Kitty called from the kitchen door, waving the baby bottle.

I finished milking Gretchen and carried the pail to the house. Kitty strained it into the bottle and set the rest aside for cheese. I stood over the stove warming my frozen hands. The house was close and stuffy, reeking of wood smoke and bacon grease. Eric was still not down.

"Go feed those lambs," Pa said, entering the kitchen with an armful of logs. He shoved Hunter aside with his boot and added more wood to the stove. "Don't let them drink too fast or they'll get colicky."

I followed my own deep tracks back to the barn, my fingers warmed by the baby bottle. Inside, the only light came from two cobweb-covered windows and a dozen windy gaps in the siding. I moved through the twilight toward the lambs. They stood in the shadows, their heads thrust through the paddock fence, bleating hungrily. I scooped up the white one, lay him across my upraised knee, and forced the bottle between his lips. He tried to break free, then got a taste of milk on his narrow pink tongue and began sucking greedily, a thin white trickle spilling from the corner of his mouth.

"Easy," I whispered, withdrawing the bottle a moment. He lunged forward, catching the nipple between his teeth. As he concentrated on the milk his legs grew slack, his heart calm. When he finished half the bottle, I set him back in the paddock and reached for his brother. But the black lamb dashed out of reach, burrowing under the straw. Twice he managed to slip through my hands before I got a secure hold. Then he peed all over my fingers.

"Don't do that!" I cried, dropping him into the straw. In an instant he slipped under the sheepcote fence and raced across an empty horse stall to a narrow gap in the siding.

"Where you gonna go in this storm?" I asked, grabbing him from behind as he tried to push his face through the windy hole. "Aren't you hungry?" I set him over my knee, pried open his jaws, and slid the nipple between his teeth, but he shook his head free. "You're ornery, aren't you?"

I tried again, stroking the curly black wool on his head, but he continued to resist, stretching his neck toward the hole in the siding, bleating loudly for his mother.

"She can't help you," I said. "Come on, you need this." Once more I forced the bottle between his teeth, then gently rubbed his throat, but the milk just ran down his neck onto my knee. "If you don't want it, your brother certainly does." When I set him down, he bounded back to the hole, sticking his nose between the cracked boards. The wind whistled around him, depositing a small mound of snow in the straw like a shaft of light.

"You'll freeze to death out there," I said, kneeling beside him. The icy wind ruffled the wool on his back. Without picking him up I held the bottle to his mouth. This time he took the nipple, quickly finishing the milk.

"Where's the ewe that had the stillborn?" Pa asked, shaking the snow from his head.

I found her in the middle of the flock, whickering for her dead lamb, her bag full of milk.

"Bring her over here," Pa ordered.

I led her to the paddock. Still hungry, the white lamb approached on unsteady legs. The ewe sniffed at him, then stepped aside, refusing to let him suck. Pa picked up the lamb and rubbed his back under the ewe's tail to give him her scent, but she was not fooled and kicked him away as soon as he neared her udder.

"We'll have to bind her legs," he said, pulling two leather thongs and a halter from the wall. While he struggled to tie her up, the wind blew open the hayloft door above us, filling the air with swirling grass and snow.

"Shut that!" Pa cried, swearing as the ewe grunted and kicked, stepping on his hands. The open door banged like a rifle shot against the outside of the barn.

I climbed up to the loft and stood at the very edge of the open bay, the snow stinging my face as I held the frame with one hand and reached out with the other, trying to pull the door closed.

"Shut that door!" Pa yelled impatiently.

"I can't. It's stuck."

"Damn!" he bellowed. "Do I have to do everything myself?"

I could feel the vibration of Pa's heavy boots

as he climbed the ladder, cursing his bad leg. I tried once more to yank the door shut, pulling so hard I lost my balance. I would have fallen from the loft had Pa not grabbed me from behind. As he did I noticed something white hanging just below me.

"You're more trouble than you're worth today," he said, pulling the door shut and tying it. "Go fetch more milk. The graft won't take. And tell Eric I want him up here now. Not next week, not this afternoon, *now!* He's got ten minutes, then I'm coming to get him myself."

When I reached the bottom of the ladder, the black lamb was again trying to nose his way through the wall. I returned him to the paddock, then left the barn, circling around to take a closer look at what was below the loft door. Hanging upside down from a large hook was the newborn lambs' mother, her mouth and eyes frozen open, her bloody wool caked with snow. I approached her slowly. I'd seen many slaughtered sheep, had even helped Pa do the killing, drawing the knife across their taut, woolly throats. It was how we made our living, Pa reminded me, how we survived. But that didn't make it any easier to watch the life slowly drain out of them, kicking and bleating with all the fury of life one minute, hanging cold and still the next, their spirit gone, nothing but wool and meat and bones. What happened to them? Where did they go when we opened their veins and let their blood spill onto the hard ground? Did they understand they were dying? Did they hate us for killing them?

I reached out and stroked the ewe's thick winter coat. "I'm sorry," I whispered, looking into the open, empty eyes. My shoulders shook violently for a moment, as though gripped by a fierce chill. I wrapped my arms around my chest and backed away. The wind calmed for a moment and in the sudden silence I heard the bleating of the black lamb. He had gotten loose again and was pushing his nose through the barn siding just below his lifeless mother.

CHAPTER

4

 Eric lay sprawled on his bed drawing, his right arm hanging over the side, his eyes darting between the window and a sketch pad on the floor.

"Pa wants you in the barn," I said, leaning against the doorjamb.

"Go away," he muttered without looking at me. I sat at the foot of my bed and watched him draw our bedroom window and the snow-covered barn it framed.

"He's real angry about the harness."

"I'm gonna fix it," Eric replied.

I waited a moment, then added, "He said if you're not up at the barn in ten minutes, he's gonna drag you there."

Eric continued to draw, ignoring me. I was afraid of what might happen. "It's almost nine o'clock," I pleaded.

"Will you leave me alone!"

"Pa needs you."

"No, he doesn't. He just wants to order me around. He could fix that harness himself in five minutes."

"You broke it."

"I said I'd fix it. It's not the only harness in the barn."

"Pa wants it done."

"And I'm busy right now."

I walked over to the window and looked up to the high pasture, where two mares and their yearling colts stood beneath a bare oak, pawing the snow in search of browse. Beyond them lay the woodlot where Pa hunted deer and wild turkey and harvested the trees we burned all winter. He would have been back there now with Dart and Doc dragging out tree trunks if it hadn't been snowing so hard.

"You're blocking the light," Eric snapped. The floor was littered with sketches of faces and hands, studies of our room, drawings of horses, dogs, and cats.

"Please get dressed," I begged, watching the barn for signs of Pa.

"You're a real pain," he barked, pushing himself up to his elbows. He paused, studying the window light as it fell across my face, then swung his long legs over the side of the bed and pulled on a pair of dirty overalls, fastening only one strap. Everything he wore was too small, but Pa said if he wanted new clothes, he'd have to earn the money to buy them.

As he trudged downstairs, Kitty blocked his path and announced, "You're not wearing those clothes one more day," her face screwed tight with disgust. "Go put on something with a little less personality."

"Would everyone get off my back," Eric complained, trying to push past her.

"The only place you're going is up," she insisted, holding her ground. She was shorter than Eric but broader.

He glared at her, then headed back up to our room. Kitty winked at me in triumph.

"They're both in a mood today, aren't they?" she said with a wry smile. "Never mind, they'll get over it."

"No, they won't."

"Don't look so worried," she said, pressing my cheeks between her fleshy palms. "Uncle Ray is not the voice of God, just a cranky old man with a bad leg. One day you're going to look at him and wonder what you found so frightening."

"He's not old," I said.

"Not yet," she replied, "but he will be one day. And then *you'll* be taking care of *him*."

"No, I won't." I might grow older, but Pa would always remain the same, making the decisions, giving the orders. "He's got a lot on his mind, you know."

"You don't have to defend him to me," she said. "I know how hard he works. But he could work just as hard with a smile on his face. It wouldn't cost him anything."

"He used to smile."

Kitty understood the unspoken thought. "Isn't it about time he stopped feeling sorry for himself? You suffered a loss, too. The three of us count for something. I don't know about you, but I'm sure worth a 'howdy' every now and again."

Pa led Dart and Doc through the blizzard toward the snowplow. "Soon as you finish with the lambs give me a hand," he shouted, tying the horses to the fence. Their bushy manes snapped furiously in the storm. They were huge horses, capable of hauling a fully loaded wagon all day, harvesting a hillside, or cutting a wide swath through two feet of wet snow as though it were nothing but mist.

I found the white lamb nursing on his adoptive mother, the tightly bound ewe unable to kick him away when he butted his head up against her bag. Though she occasionally squirmed and grunted, he was more determined to suck than she was to be left alone. Pa was wrong; the graft would take. But the black lamb didn't make the same effort. He lay buried in the straw, bleating weakly. When I picked him up, he took the bottle. "If you're that hungry, try suckling," I said, setting him under the ewe. But he would not drink from her. So I gave him the rest of the bottle and went out to help Pa.

"Take the lines and back them into the traces," he said. In his rush to get the horses hitched, he had forgotten his threat to pull Eric out of bed. I backed them against the snowplow and chained them to the shaft.

"Step lively, lads," Pa called. Ahead of us everything had fused together in an endless white sea. The heavy plow rumbled over the frozen earth, scraping it clean. We drove past the house, through the pine grove, and out to the Providence road.

"Town better get plowing or we're outta business," Pa said, looking down the steep hill. We sold a lot of lambs and wool in winter, but only when Pa was able to make deliveries and receive customers.

He handed me the reins and climbed down, walking behind the plow, checking the blade. "That's good," he called. It was the first time he'd let me handle it alone. I turned around and smiled. Pa rarely offered praise. "Keep your eyes forward," he scolded. "Take them up as high as the barn, then come down on the opposite side." As we passed the house, Pa headed inside. My chest grew tight; he hadn't forgotten his threat after all.

By the time I turned around and headed back out to the road, the brown swath we had plowed was already white. The sleigh rumbled downhill; snow blew in my face. Bianca passed overhead, settling in a tall spruce at the end of the drive.

When I reached her, she leapt from the tree and soared out over the valley, banking and dipping, buffeted by the fierce winds. For just a moment, in the midst of the storm, I felt a sense of warmth I had not felt since Mama left.

But the sound of shouting shattered it.

"I said *now!*" Pa bellowed.

I turned the horses around and hurried back to the house. Eric stood beside the woodpile, jacket unbuttoned, boots unlaced, his hands in his pockets.

"And when you're finished, chop this wood."

"Stop bullying him, Uncle Ray," Kitty said, standing in the door.

"Keep out of this," he snapped.

"Get nasty with me, and you'll be eating cold mutton for a month," she threatened.

Eric turned and trudged up to the barn, looking more annoyed at being defended by Kitty than yelled at by Pa.

"No harness, no lunch," Pa called after him. "And you better do a good job."

Eric didn't come in for lunch. Pa ate without speaking, without tasting, it seemed, then slammed his fork down and left the table, determined to see if Eric had done as he was told.

"You haven't finished your food, Uncle Ray," Kitty called after him.

"I've had all I can stomach," he shot back.

"No one can hold a candle to Burnses for

stubbornness," she reflected, grabbing her shawl and boots. I watched from the kitchen as Kitty hurried out into the snow. By the time she reached the barn, Pa was coming back out, the broken harness slung over his arm.

Eric was gone. The harness hadn't been touched.

We ate dinner in silence, just the three of us, then Pa went up to bed, something he only did when his leg was paining him real bad.

"You think Eric's all right?" I asked Kitty as we cleared the dishes.

"Your brother can take care of himself," she answered, rolling up her sleeves. "Isn't that what he's always telling us?"

"It's freezing out."

"One cold night might help him appreciate what he's got here." She seemed as annoyed with Eric as she was with Pa.

"Are you sorry you came to live with us?"

"No, I'm not sorry," she said with surprise. "All families have their troubles."

When we finished washing the dishes, Kitty sat down at Mama's piano. "This came in yesterday's mail," she said, pulling a sheet of music from a large envelope. Whenever Kitty had a few extra dollars, she sent away for piano music.

"Listen," she said, beginning to play a sort of lullaby, her thick fingers pressing the keys with surprising softness. After a short introduction she added her voice, singing in another language, the words floating through the room. Hunter got up from the stove and set himself down near the piano pedals. When she finished, her eyes glistened. "Well, what do you think?"

"It was nice," I said flatly.

"Nice? Nathan, don't be so dull. That's Bach, Johann Sebastian Bach, the greatest musician that ever lived. Wasn't it sublime?"

"What did the words mean?"

"Sleep, o weary eyes, gently and blessed."

"That's all?"

"Forget the words," she scolded. "Did it speak to you here?" She tapped my breastbone with her forefinger. "Did you feel anything special? Did it bring tears to your eyes?"

I shook my head.

"Heathen! Music is the best medicine there is for gloom. Wouldn't hurt your pa to get a good dose now and again." She left the piano and stood by the window. "The wind's died down." The snow continued to fall but now seemed more blessing than burden, quietly blanketing the earth.

"Come with me," she said, slipping on her shawl and stepping outside. The light from the kitchen lamp threw a dull yellow rectangle across the dooryard. Large white flakes drifted through the curtain of light and came to rest on the waist-high drifts. The driveway looked as though it hadn't been plowed. "Isn't it beautiful?" Kitty whispered.

"I hope Eric's all right," I said, picturing him shivering somewhere in the woods or up in the empty cabin.

"He'll be fine."

We walked around the side of the house and looked across the valley. The Hejdlings' house twinkled brightly, every window lit with electric light. "Doesn't that look cheery?" she mused. "No reason we can't live like that. It's the twentieth century. Uncle Ray ought to buy himself a tractor, replace that leaky icebox with an electric refrigerator, get one of those new radios. Times are changing."

"He'd never do any of that."

"No, I don't suppose so. How are the lambs?"

"The lambs! They need another bottle."

"I thought you grafted them."

"Only one," I said, hurrying back inside.

"Boots!" Kitty cried. I kicked them off, filled the baby bottle with what remained of the goats' milk, pulled the boots back on, then ran to the barn.

I felt my way through the dark to the tack room and lit the lamp, sending long, flickering fingers of light across the dirt floor. The barn was oddly silent, as though more than Eric had fled. I found the sheep bedded down for the night, all facing the closed door to the corral. The white lamb lay nestled against the warm wool of his adopted mother. When the light fell across him he stirred, found the ewe's teat, and began to suck in his sleep. The ewe never awoke. His stubborn brother lay where I had left him, looking half frozen. I slipped him inside my jacket and put the bottle in his mouth. He seemed too weak to suck. I squeezed a few drops onto his tongue and gradually he revived, growing warmer. As soon as he finished the bottle, he fell asleep inside my jacket.

It was then, in the absolute stillness, that I realized Bianca was gone. I held the lamp aloft, searching the shadows for her, but the rafters were bare. "Bianca," I whispered. Nothing stirred. I clung to the sleeping lamb and carried him down to the house for the night.

CHAPTER

5

Shortly after midnight I awoke to the creak of floorboards in the hall.

"Eric?" I whispered.

Pa stood in the doorway, peering through the darkness at the empty bed. The black lamb stirred, hidden beneath the covers. I held his mouth shut.

"Where's Eric?" I asked.

"Go back to sleep," Pa said. He wore an extra sweater against the cold and carried an unlit hurricane lamp that clanged against his leg as he left the doorway and walked downstairs. A minute later the back door clicked and a faint yellow light flickered against the windowpane. I dragged the quilt to the window and watched Pa cross the barnyard, wondering what he would do when he discovered one of the lambs missing. We weren't allowed to bring them into the house. Pa said it made them soft. Even the cats had to winter in the barn. They learned to mouse much better that way. Only old Hunter was allowed inside.

But Pa didn't enter the barn, he limped past it, head buried in his collar. The yellow flame crossed the upper pasture and disappeared into the woods.

My bare feet stung with cold as I kept vigil by the window. Hunter ambled up the stairs, sniffed at the lamb asleep against my chest, put his front paws on Eric's bed, then pulled one of his shirts from a chair and lay down upon it. My eyes grew heavy. I tried to stave off sleep by humming to myself, shifting my weight from one leg to the other, but finally returned to bed, lying knotted inside the quilt, knees pressed to my chest, the lamb against my face.

I dreamt that Eric stood outside trying to get back into the house, but all the doors and windows had been nailed shut. I shouted for Pa to help, but he was up in the pasture breaking the colts. I finally managed to pry open our bedroom window, but when I leaned out to help him up, I lost my balance and fell. My arms jerked forward to break my fall. The motion woke me.

I looked across at Eric's bed, then at the window. The snow fell more lightly. I heard footsteps and my heart leapt. *Was Eric back?* Pa trod heavily up the steps and past my door, the lamplight briefly filling the room. Then his door snapped shut and the house grew silent. I listened for Eric.

Nothing stirred. Leaving the sleeping lamb inside my bedcovers, I crept across the hall, knocked softly on Pa's door, and opened it. He sat at Mama's writing table, absentmindedly chewing the end of a pencil as he stared at the darkened window. The lamp lit the underside of his stubbly chin.

"What are you doing up?" he muttered.

"Did you find Eric?"

"Get back to bed."

"Was he up at the cabin?"

Pa shook his head.

"Where is he?"

"He can take care of himself."

"What if he's hurt? He could freeze to death out there."

"I raised tougher sons than that," Pa said. "He may be stubborn—he comes by that honestly enough—but he's not stupid."

"Where do you think he went?"

"I followed his tracks to the logging trail. He headed toward Providence. Now back to bed."

"Aren't you going to sleep?"

"I've got some thinking to do yet."

"Could I stay with you awhile?" I asked. The house felt so empty without Eric. Kitty slept behind the kitchen, too far away to be a comfort in the dark. Pa usually had no patience with my night fears, but this once he pushed himself back from the desk and pulled me between his knees. His fingers were cold and hard. He brushed the hair from my face, then laid his hands on my shoulders and looked into my eyes.

"You used to favor your mama," he said, his voice just above a whisper. He wrapped his fingers around my upper arms. "I was just as spindly at your age but strong. I was gonna be as good as my brothers if it killed me, better even. And I was. I learned from their mistakes."

He released my arms. "Don't be like your brother."

"I'm not," I protested.

He smiled ruefully. "You're a good boy, Nathan. Someday you'll make a fine farmer."

He looked past me to the window.

"I've tried to be a good father to you boys." His voice was heavy with regret. "I had no pa to study from. I meant to set you boys on your own two feet early so you could take care of yourselves if need be. It's hard enough farming without having to train someone to it night and day, worse when they run off without putting all that training to good use. Times are hard.

"A man counts on a few things in life beyond himself, the fewer the better. In the beginning you think you can do it all. You work for others like a slave, saving every dime, dreaming of the time you'll be able to buy your freedom, a place of your own. Ten years pass, maybe more. You find a farm. It may not be what you dreamt of, but it's what you can afford. You scrape together enough for a down payment. But after all that, you don't really own the place, the bank does. Suddenly you've got a partner you swore you'd never have. But without the bank you couldn't afford to buy the land, the livestock, the seed. It's a bitter pill, but you swallow it, telling yourself you'll make no further compromises. It helps to look out over your pastures, smack the flanks of your horses, dream of the time you'll own it free and clear.

"The first years are hard. You're too impatient. Wiser folks say you should hold off another three weeks before spring planting. But you take a chance, hoping for the first crop and the best price. Ten days later frost wipes you out. You got to start over, borrow more money, get deeper into debt.

"After three, four years, you think you've got it licked. You understand the land now, the weather, the animals, your own limitations. You'll never grow rich, but you didn't expect to. It's enough just to be your own boss, work your own land. You step outside one spring morning and feel the earth warming beneath your feet, smell the new grass, hear the sheep, the goats, the horses, and you think to yourself: *A few years ago there was nothing here but an empty, weather-beaten barn and a tumbledown house*. And now look, a whole new world that didn't exist before you came—sixty, seventy animals in a place that was nothing but weeds.

"Suddenly you take it into your head to find

yourself a wife, start a family. You've changed. It's no longer enough to work for yourself alone. You want to share it with someone who'll cook your meals, mend your clothes, warm your bed; someone who'll give you the children you'll need as the farm grows and you get too old to work it."

Pa's eyes left the window and returned to mine.

"But it doesn't always work out that way. Marriages that begin in love sometimes end in misery. Children grow up and decide to follow their own dreams. And meanwhile, you keep changing. One morning you wake up and find the fire inside your soul has died. You drag yourself out of bed as though hobbled by the influenza. Life suddenly feels empty, just an endless, exhausting round of chores, day after day, season after season, year after year. Your muscles ache, your back grows stiff, you don't sleep well, you take no pleasure in work or rest or food. You look for someone to blame: the bank for taking so much of your hard-earned profits, your children for caring so little about your dream, your wife for siding with your children and failing to understand that you did it all for her and for them.

"In anger you say, 'Go then, just leave me be. I did it alone before; I can do it again.' But when they leave, you realize they've also taken your soul. All that remains is the labor, the back-breaking, pitiless labor. You keep your head down, focused on what lies immediately underfoot. You grow hard as stone, cold as ice."

He stopped and rubbed his face.

"I'm not gonna leave you, Pa."

"That's what Eric said when he was your age."

"I'm not Eric," I insisted.

"True enough," he whispered, drawing me in against his chest. He held me tight a moment, kissed the top of my head, then sent me back to bed.

CHAPTER

6

Pa wasn't down for breakfast the next morning. I found the kitchen empty and ice-cold, a meager winter light sifting through the windows. I stoked the fire, set water to boil, then retrieved the lamb from my room, hoping to return him to the barn before Pa found out. Hunter followed me to the back door but hesitated when he saw the wall of snow outside. I grabbed the shovel and cleared a path, but when I went to pick up the lamb, he scurried out of reach under the sofa. Kitty found me trying to coax him out with a bottle.

"Contrary little thing." She smiled. "Just like a Burns. He'll come out when he's hungry."

"What if Pa sees him?"

"Wouldn't do any harm to have some new life around here, especially this little rebel. Better see to Gretchen."

When I came in for breakfast, Pa still wasn't

down. "He's worse than Eric," Kitty said. Her left cheek dimpled in a sardonic smile.

"He was up late last night," I explained.

"How would you know?"

"We talked awhile."

"These truly are remarkable times. If I get five words out of your father in a week, I consider myself lucky. You all need to open your mouths more, let your hearts out. You tiptoe around like there's a corpse in the next room."

Kitty mashed the remains of last night's potatoes into a frying pan, then threw in a spoonful of butter and an onion. "I never thought I'd see the day your father overslept."

"Maybe he's not feeling well."

"In this weather anything's possible, even remorse. Go tell him if he wants his hash browns hot, he better get himself down here in the next five minutes."

But Pa wasn't in his room. From the look of it, he'd never gone to bed.

"Pa's gone out," I said coming down the stairs.

"Gone and back again," Kitty replied, pointing out the window. He rode slowly up the drive astride Dart.

When he came through the door, Kitty said, "Did you find him?"

Pa sat down without speaking, his face a strange mixture of anger, exhaustion, and relief.

"Uncle Ray, this is the last meal you'll eat from my hands if you don't fess up quick and tell us how Eric is. You think you're the only one who didn't sleep last night for worrying about him?"

He picked up his fork and began eating.

Kitty turned to me and said, "I guess what we ought to do is look in on the Hejdlings after breakfast. Perhaps they know something we don't."

When Pa finished he pushed his plate aside and said, "Clean out his bureau and desk."

"Excuse me?" Kitty asked, winking at me.

"Take his clothes," he snapped, "and those damn paints and brushes."

"Where exactly would you like us to take them?"

Pa pointed across the valley to the Hejdlings' farm.

As I hitched the horses to the sleigh, Bianca fluttered into the barn and settled on her favorite perch, cooing loudly, her presence somehow easing the stinging cold that had filled the place since Eric's disappearance.

"Welcome back," I said, my spirits brightening.

Pa came out and tossed his sheepskin vest in the back of the sleigh. "It's too tight for me," he said, then returned to the house.

As I handed Kitty into the sleigh, Hunter jumped up behind us, nestling beside Eric's clothes.

"Get back inside," I scolded.

"Let him be," Kitty said looking over her

shoulder. "He misses Eric, too. He'd never run out on your brother without saying good-bye, God knows. I wonder at that boy sometimes. He's got some fine qualities, but family feeling isn't one of them."

We drove out to the road and turned down the narrow white ribbon that plunged sharply toward Providence, the sun reflecting from every surface. The runners glided along the hard-packed surface, whistling in the cold air. I held the horses back, calling out as Pa would, "Easy, lads, easy."

"Don't you feel like you've just been released from prison?" Kitty asked, stretching out her arms and breathing deeply. "Look how beautiful everything is." Her eyes glittered. "Not a cloud in the sky."

Halfway down the hill we crossed a small wooden bridge spanning Providence Creek. Kitty asked me to stop. The black water cut a channel through the snow, tinkling as it fell over the rocks.

"Isn't that the most soothing sound?"

"Better than Bach?" I asked with a smile.

"One and the same," she declared.

From there the Hejdling farm seemed close enough to touch, the lower house just above the road, the barn a few hundred yards farther up, then the main house, all three buildings gleaming a spotless white. At the bottom of the hill, we turned off onto the Hejdlings' road and climbed to the main house, Kitty admiring the well-kept buildings.

As we pulled up to the front door, Mr. Hejdling emerged wearing a dark suit, the sun glinting off his white hair. He came down the shoveled steps and helped Kitty from the sleigh. Hunter sat up on the backseat, wagging his tail fiercely.

"Thank you for taking in my cousin during that awful blizzard," Kitty began.

"Glad to be of help. And how are you, young man?" he asked, shaking my hand. His fingernails were clean and neatly trimmed, not chipped and dirty like Pa's. "You've grown a foot or more since I saw you last. Bittle tells me you're doing the harvesting now." I nodded. "It's a great comfort to have a son in harness."

Bittle appeared at the front door, holding a piece of dark blue eggshell. His pockets were always filled with curiosities he'd discovered in the woods. Mr. Hejdling told him to stable and water our horses. Bittle grinned, stowed the eggshell in his jacket, then unhitched the horses and led them away while we followed his father inside.

The Hejdling house was as neat and spacious as ours was dark and cluttered, the floors covered in fine rugs, the walls hung with paintings and tapestries. Mr. Hejdling led us to a small study, asked if we would join him for coffee, then stepped back into the hall to call his daughters. Kitty ran her hand over the sofa and the polished mahogany coffee table. Mr. Hejdling returned, followed by Lisa, who carried a tray of coffee cups and cake. She set it down without looking at us, then left. She seemed annoyed.

"Your brother is quite independent-minded, isn't he?" Mr. Hejdling asked, sitting forward on a stiff-backed chair to pour the coffee. "I wish I had had half his confidence at that age."

"He's a talented boy," Kitty explained.

"So I hear."

Kitty accepted a plate of cake. "My uncle is not a great patron of the arts."

"I appreciate his dilemma," Mr. Hejdling said, taking only coffee for himself. "It's hard to run a farm alone."

Sonja came to the door. Her father motioned her into the room with an outstretched hand. "Come in, say hello."

Sonja entered wearing her dark blue school dress and wool leggings, her blond hair neatly parted in the center and gathered at the back in a single thick braid. She bowed before Kitty but ignored me, taking the chair beside the sofa. The light from the window danced in her eyes as she followed the discussion between Kitty and her father.

"As I told your uncle this morning," Mr. Hejdling explained, "I have no wish to come between father and son. As long as Mr. Burns does not object, Eric is welcome to remain here, provided he keeps up with his chores and lessons. It's a bitter day when father and son part company this way."

"When their mother died—," Kitty began.

"You needn't explain," Mr. Hejdling interrupted with a raised hand. "I know only too well what such tragedies can do to a family."

"Of course you do," Kitty replied softly.

Mr. Hejdling stroked the back of his daughter's head. "The girls seemed to take the loss better than the boys," he reflected. "I would have thought otherwise. I suppose women are more acceptant of fate, men too accustomed to controlling it, or believing they can."

Kitty turned to Sonja. "Maybe one evening you and your sister would like to come up and have supper with us."

"We have to take care of Papa," Sonja said into her hands.

"Perhaps he could spare you for a few hours some Sunday afternoon for tea."

"I'm sure they'd be delighted," Mr. Hejdling replied, turning to his daughter. "I encourage them to get out, especially Lisa. It's time she started giving thought to her future. This one here has a little time yet." He kissed her cheek, then told her to go help her sister in the kitchen.

"She's a beauty," Kitty remarked after she left.

"And a handful," he replied, turning to me. "I'm sure you don't give your father half the worry she gives me." He ran his hand over his head. "Most of these white hairs are her doing."

"I don't expect you'll see any softening in Eric," Kitty said. "But if he should seem open to the idea of returning home . . ."

"Perhaps you should speak with him," Mr. Hejdling suggested.

Bittle went to fetch Eric, who entered wearing yesterday's clothes and a look of stubborn determination. He stood by the doorway, refusing Mr. Hejdling's offer of a seat, eyes fixed on the window.

"Eric, if you're going to board in my house," Mr. Hejdling explained firmly, "we'll have to understand each other from the outset. I expect to be heeded by my hired hands no less than by my children. I'm not your father, I'm your employer. If you want to hold on to this job, you'd better do as bidden. I won't ask a second time."

Eric moved into the room slowly, taking the seat Sonja had vacated. Outside, Hunter began to bark.

"Do you have anything you'd care to say to Miss Kitty or your brother? They've brought your things."

"Thanks," he said flatly, clearly annoyed by our presence.

Mr. Hejdling excused himself, shutting the door behind him. We sat in silence, Eric glaring at the window, Kitty studying him with puzzled eyes.

"We brought your art supplies as well," Kitty explained.

Eric said nothing.

"I'm not gonna take sides in this," Kitty tried again, "but you should know—"

"Don't tell me what I should know," he interrupted. "Just leave me alone, go back where you came from. Who are you anyway?"

"Your cousin," Kitty said calmly. "I care about what happens to you. So does your father. He loves you in his way."

"He sent you his sheepskin vest," I said, hoping the gift would please him. He glared at me without responding.

"He's granted you your freedom," Kitty added. "Don't hurt him any more than you already have."

"Hurt *him!* What about me? He hates me."

"He doesn't hate you, Eric. He just doesn't understand you."

Eric walked over to the window. Hunter caught sight of him and resumed his barking.

"Hunter misses you," I said.

"Why don't you both just go home," he said, turning and leaving the room.

Before we left, Kitty stopped in the kitchen to deliver a bag of yarn to Gregory's pregnant wife. The oldest son, Halvard, entered the room in search of his father, greeted Kitty, then shook my hand. He was as fair as his two sisters and as squarely built as his father but shorter than Gregory.

When Mr. Hejdling led us back to the sleigh, Kitty asked him to let us know the moment Eric had outstayed his welcome. "We would hate for him to become a burden."

"I'll take every opportunity to encourage him to return home, where he's needed most," he said. "You'll hear from me if there's any change."

I glanced toward our ridge. Our weather-beaten barn looked abandoned compared to the Hejdlings'. I realized then how hard it was for Pa to keep at it, sunup to sunset, never achieving even a fraction of the success his nearest neighbor had. And now he faced the task with one less pair of hands.

CHAPTER

7

The next few weeks Pa kept to himself, saying little, eating without appetite, ignoring Kitty whenever she tried to prod him into discussing Eric. The first time Rebel escaped from my room, Pa barely took notice, saying, "You'll runt him with all your fussing." In the past he would have tossed him out the door. After that, Rebel had the run of the house. He nosed around Hunter's scraps, bleated for milk, and slept at the foot of my bed. Kitty smiled whenever she saw him.

Up in the barn we released the ewe from the birthing paddock and put her in with the other mothers. The white lamb grew quickly and was soon running with the flock. I took Rebel up to the barn every morning, where he played with his brother and nibbled at the feed bin so long as I remained in view; but the moment I headed back to the house or up to the pasture, he slipped under the fence and ran after me.

Pa went about his work mutely, making even the animals uncomfortable. Whenever he entered the barn, the sheep hurried from the sheepcote, bounding out into the snow. Bianca retreated to a distant corner, huddling silently in the darkness until he left. Out in the pasture the mares and colts snorted and stamped as he approached, then bolted for the woods.

The third week in January the snow returned, falling lightly, a steady, foglike drizzle that whitened the muddy barnyard and corral. Twice a day I loaded the hay sled, hitched it to Dart, and rode up to the pasture to feed the horses. The colts loved the snow, dashing across the field. I could feel the pounding of their hooves underfoot as I passed through the pasture gate, their nostrils blowing streams of smoke in the freezing air.

As I made my late-afternoon run the third day of the snow, the sheep slipped under the corral railing, passed through a hole in the pasture fence, and proceeded in a nearly straight line to the top of the frozen meadow. There they turned to face the setting sun, invisible behind a dull white sky. I unloaded the snow-whitened hay, then watched the horses amble toward me. I would have let them spend the night in the barn, but Pa said they wintered better out of doors. "Cold's much tougher on them after they've gotten used to being warm," he insisted.

Across the valley the Hejdlings' cows began their slow journey back to the barn, lowing as they walked, bells clanging. A solitary figure followed behind, carrying a switch that he used to encourage the stragglers. The heavy, awkward gait and slightly hunched shoulders looked like Eric's. I cupped my hands to my mouth and yelled his name, waving my arms to attract his attention. If he heard me, a mile and a half away, he didn't bother to look up. But Bianca did, leaving her perch under the barn roof and settling on the hay sled, where she pecked at the loose grain.

The gray sky turned indigo, the pasture melting into the trees. In the gathering darkness the sheep headed back to the barn, bleating for supper. The white lamb hurried after them, his new mother giving him a push whenever he fell behind. One of the colts left the hay and trotted over to play with him, but mother and child dashed toward the center of the flock for protection, the ewe kicking her short legs out behind her in an effort to discourage the horse's attentions.

As I turned to follow them, a small herd of deer appeared at the edge of the pasture sniffing the air, their beige bodies blending into the bare trees. One by one they dropped their heads and began to feed, digging through the snow with their sharp, heart-shaped hooves. Every few moments a narrow head rose, ears outstretched, scanning the darkness for signs of danger, then returned to the ground.

The light vanished, leaving only the glow from the twinkling barn across the valley and Kitty's kitchen lamp. I brushed the remaining hay from the sled, looking one last time in the direction of the deer, now nearly invisible against the trees. Once again a pair of antlers shot upright, listening, but this time the deer turned and bounded for cover, his white tail raised in alarm. The others quickly followed, snapping twigs as they vanished into the woods. At the same moment Bianca leapt into the air and flew back to the safety of the barn.

"What is it?" I called after her, my skin tingling.

Dart raised his head and stopped chewing. Then two of the colts ran to the lower end of the pasture. The mares followed, abandoning the hay. Suddenly the black pasture seemed alive with menace. I climbed upon Dart's high back for protection, took hold of the reins, and turned him toward the barn, looking over my shoulder at the upper corner of pasture. Something moved up there, stalking so low to the ground I could make out only a black shoulder or back. "Hurry, Dart," I said, digging my heels into his ribs. He broke into a canter, the empty sled bouncing wildly behind. At the fence I scrambled to the ground, my heart pounding, sensing danger behind every rock and tree. I yanked Dart through the gate, urging him forward in hoarse whispers, then leapt onto his back and dashed to the barn.

"Boots!" Kitty yelled as I burst through the door panting, the barn lamp in my hand. Pa looked around from his desk.

"I think I just saw a bear," I said, trembling.

"Take the lamp back to the barn," he replied.

"Where?" Kitty asked, setting the table for supper.

"Top of the pasture. I couldn't really tell. It was too dark."

"Hasn't been a bear around here in fifty years," Pa said. "Too much open pasture."

"What was it, then?" Kitty asked.

"His own shadow, most likely. Lamp."

"Let him eat his dinner first," Kitty said. "Wash up." I was relieved not to have to go back out in the dark just yet.

After supper Pa grabbed the lamp and walked it back to the barn. A few minutes later he called to me.

"You count the sheep before you came in?" he asked. He held the lamp high, lighting the dark pen.

In my terror I had forgotten. The ewes often gave birth in distant corners of the farm, wandering into the woods or behind a rock to have their lambs. When the count came up short, we went looking for them. Sometimes they did just fine on their own, mother and baby joining the flock the next morning. Sometimes they didn't, and if we failed to reach them in time, all we found were their cold carcasses.

"How many you count now?" Pa asked.

"Sixty-five," I said after a moment.

"How many are there supposed to be?" he snapped.

"Sixty-six," I muttered.

"And you know which one's missing, don't you."

"Yes, sir." I braced myself, expecting to be cuffed. But Pa stayed strangely calm.

"If you'd counted them at twilight, we'd have had a fighting chance of finding her. It's nearly impossible in the dark."

"I think I know where she is," I said.

"Where are you both going?" Kitty called from the back door as we left the barn.

"Ewe's missing," I shouted to her.

"I don't like you being out there with something moving about in the dark. Uncle Ray!"

Pa ignored her, heading around the barn toward the gate. I pointed through the darkness to the far corner of the pasture. Kitty hurried after us with a second lamp. The snow crackled underfoot. Pa limped ahead, eyes fixed on the spot. Where I'd fed the horses, he stopped and turned his ear into the wind. When I began to walk on, he grabbed hold of my collar and growled, "Don't move," then dowsed his lamp and motioned to Kitty to do the same. For a moment the night seemed solid darkness, but as our eyes adjusted, the line separating field from trees came clear and up in the far corner that line moved.

"Is that the ewe?" Kitty asked.

"Quiet!" he whispered. "She's not alone."

Terror flooded back over me.

"Is it a bear?" I whispered.

"Don't think so," Pa replied, walking forward slowly.

"Back in the house," Kitty whispered. "Both of you. It's not safe."

Pa kept on going.

"At least get your gun," she said.

"Can't shoot what you can't see," he replied, walking more boldly now.

"Pa, don't," I called, watching the distance between us increase.

"Uncle Ray, don't be foolish."

"Hold your tongue," he snapped. "Both of you."

He walked on, blending into the night.

"Sounds like something sliding over the snow," Kitty whispered to me.

Pa stopped, reached into his pocket for a match, and relit his lamp, holding it high above his head. Two incandescent cat eyes gleamed out of the darkness like windowpanes reflecting a distant fire. I jumped back in fright.

"Son of a bitch," Pa growled, lunging forward on his bad leg. In the same instant a mountain lion rose up from the snow, its round, striped face stained red. It growled once, then turned and leapt into the woods.

"Damn, damn, damn," Pa muttered, hopping awkwardly up the hill.

"What in God's name was that?" Kitty asked. Pa kept cursing as the fingers of lamplight reached the motionless carcass of the missing ewe. Kitty and I hung back.

"Is she dead?" Kitty asked.

"She and the lamb both," Pa replied, walking around them. "Come here, Nathan."

"Don't, Uncle Ray," Kitty cried, covering her mouth.

"If you want to be a sheep farmer, you've got to be able to identify what's killing your flock. Come take a look at this."

I approached slowly, passing through a long streak of bloodstained snow. The ewe lay on her side, belly torn open, her unborn lamb beside her. Pa held the lantern near the ewe's neck.

"That's how they kill." He pointed to a great gash at the throat. "Then they drag their prey toward cover and gut 'em before they feed." The mountain lion had nearly finished the gutting but had not yet begun to tear into the meat.

"Will it return?" Kitty asked from a distance.

"Soon as we leave the pasture. It's probably no more than a few yards inside those trees, waiting as patient as stone." He spoke with admiration, not anger.

"Then you've got to shoot it," she declared,

holding her lantern up to illuminate the woods.

"You'll never find it," Pa insisted. "They can conceal themselves on a barren plain."

"We're not safe here so long as it's alive."

"It's not the least bit interested in us," he scoffed. "Deer's what it likes most. Sheep when necessary." He kicked the warm carcass over and studied the teeth marks. The unborn lamb was still partially enclosed in its birth sac, dangling a red-and-white umbilical cord.

"I'm sorry," I whispered to Pa and the ewe.

"Everyone makes mistakes," Kitty said in my defense.

"And this is the price you pay," Pa snapped. He knelt beside the ewe, carefully examining the pelt, then told me to grab it by the hind legs and drag it to the barn. "No sense letting a perfectly good hide go to waste."

I took hold of the legs, feeling the narrow bones through the compacted wool.

"What about the baby?" Kitty asked. "You can't just leave it here."

"I've got no use for it," Pa snapped.

"That awful animal will eat it."

"Let it."

"I'm not leaving it here," Kitty declared. "I couldn't sleep thinking of it." She held her lamp before her and slowly approached the little mound.

"Leave it be," Pa called. "You can't fight nature."

"Oh yes, you can." Tears stood in her angry eyes. She wrapped the three-pound baby in her shawl and lifted it with both hands like a sacrificial offering. Pa walked away in disgust.

"I'm sorry," I muttered.

"Wasn't your fault," she said, looking down at the lifeless bundle in her hands.

～ We kept careful watch for the mountain lion after that, counting the sheep twice a day, but saw no further sign of it. During the January thaw we sheared the flock, filling the barnyard with mountains of dirty gray wool, which Kitty gathered into great burlap bags to be washed, carded, and spun. She thought it cruel to strip the sheep of their heavy coats in midwinter, but Pa said we needed two crops a year to pay the bills and insisted the cold helped the wool grow back quickly. "I'll bet it does," she said, grasping her arms to her chest.

All but the nursing ewes and lambs were shorn as the snow turned to slush, their bulky bodies made sleek and pink in minutes. Burlap bags filled every corner of the house, lying under tables and chairs and atop the sofa and piano. Rebel liked to burrow inside them, scattering the loose wool across the floor like snow. Outside, the freshly shorn sheep turned yellow overnight.

"Lanolin," Pa explained, referring to the natural cream that kept them warm until the wool grew in. Against the setting sun they gleamed like molten gold.

After the shearing we took to the woods, spending most of February felling trees for firewood and fence posts, hauling the huge trunks out of the forest behind Dart and Doc, then sawing and splitting them into stove lengths. I worked in constant fear of the mountain lion, uneasy every time we entered the forest or took feed up to the mares.

The first bright Sunday in February we received an unexpected visit. Pa and I were repairing the goat shed when the sound of sleigh bells turned our eyes to the drive. The Hejdlings approached the house, Halvard and Sonja sitting up front, Lisa, alone in the back, all three wrapped in elegant Sunday coats, fur hats, and woolen scarves. Their faces glowed in the frozen air.

Annoyed, Pa dropped his tools, wiped his hands on his overalls, and trudged reluctantly toward them. Kitty came to the door, one hand feeling about her head, making sure her hair was tidy, the other brushing loose wool from her apron.

"Father sends his greetings," Halvard announced, stepping down from the sleigh and extending his hand. "I hope we're not disturbing you."

Pa looked at his own filthy hand a moment, then shook Halvard's. Kitty filled the awkward silence. "Of course you're not disturbing us, come in." Halvard bowed slightly in her direction, then helped his sisters down. He wore polished riding boots and a black woolen coat that reached to his ankles. He always dressed with care.

"We won't stay but a minute," he insisted, communicating Pa's discomfort to his sisters with a swift motion of his eyes.

"Nonsense," Kitty replied. "I've got water on for tea and fresh muffins cooling."

Sonja jumped from the front seat without taking her brother's hand, her long braid slapping against her back.

"I had a premonition about visitors today," Kitty continued, holding the door as Lisa passed wordlessly into the house.

"Go ahead," Pa said to me, trudging back to the goat shed. Kitty frowned, then hurried after our guests.

"Please forgive the mess," she apologized, removing the burlap bags from the sofa and chairs. "The sheep produced almost as much wool this winter as we've had snow." Only Halvard chuckled.

Sonja took a large uncarded clump in her hand and rubbed it against her cheek. "It's so soft," she said, handing it to her sister. Lisa refused it with a frown.

"Please sit," Kitty insisted, bustling about the

parlor. "How is Trudy? Did she have the baby?"

"One of the reasons for our visit," Halvard announced, taking a chair and unbuttoning his long coat. He had begun to grow a mustache, a nearly invisible blond fringe that he continually smoothed with thumb and forefinger. "I've got a little nephew."

"Isn't that wonderful! What's his name? Nathan, take their coats."

"Ethan," Halvard declared proudly.

"And how is Trudy feeling?"

Lisa removed her hat, shaking out her blond hair over a white blouse fastened at the neck with a silver brooch. She avoided my eyes as I took her coat, looking only at her brother.

"She and the baby are doing fine," Halvard said, watching Kitty move about the room.

"And Gregory?"

"Walking on air." Halvard crossed one thick leg over the other, tucking his tight-fitting pants into his boot top. "He's fathered a little god, you know, the perfect son."

Kitty laughed, then excused herself, hurrying to the kitchen, her hands rising to her hair as she passed the hall mirror. Sonja and Lisa exchanged looks after she left, but when they sought Halvard's eyes, he averted his gaze.

I carried the coats to Kitty's room, accidentally setting Rebel free. He bounded through the open door to the kitchen.

"Who let you out?" Kitty asked, picking him up. I carried the tea tray into the parlor. She followed holding Rebel.

"How cute!" Sonja cried. "Can I hold him?"

"He's not house-trained," Kitty warned.

"I don't care," she said, taking him in her lap. But Rebel would not be held. He squeezed through her fingers and dropped heavily to the floor. Sonja crawled under the piano to pet him.

"Father has decided to throw a little party in honor of his grandson a week from Sunday," Halvard announced as Kitty handed him a cup of tea. "He'd love you all to help us celebrate. Will you come?" For just an instant their eyes met and Kitty's face reddened.

"We'd be delighted," she stammered. Lisa scrutinized them both, setting her teacup aside without drinking.

"How is Eric?" Kitty asked, passing around the muffins.

"He couldn't have come at a better time. With Gregory mooning over Ethan all day long, we're lucky to have an extra pair of hands. Eric works hard but doesn't seem to take much joy in it."

"Like father, like son," Kitty muttered.

"I hate his eyes," Sonja suddenly declared.

"They soak up everything, don't they?" Halvard added, trying to soften her observation.

"He's always studying us," Sonja complained.

"That's what artists do," Kitty explained.

"My little sister will not be trifled with," Halvard observed. Then pointing toward the stack of piano music, he asked, "Do you play?"

"A little," Kitty admitted.

"Play for us," he pressed.

"Well, I . . . really, I'm so out of practice, and with all the carding, my fingers are so stiff."

"Just a little something," he begged. "The only music in our house these days is the sound of Ethan howling, and that tune gets a little wearying after a while."

"How about the song you sang for me," I suggested.

"Which one?" she asked, reddening.

"That lullaby."

"Perfect," Halvard reflected. "Something you could teach us to sing to Ethan."

"I . . . well . . . but the piano, it's so out of tune."

"Please," Halvard insisted, leaning forward in his chair. Lisa looked away in disgust.

Kitty rose self-consciously and walked to the piano, smoothing her dress and hair, clearing her throat.

"I'm really not—"

"No excuses," Halvard insisted.

Kitty opened the music and began to play, tiny beads of sweat gathering on her forehead. Her voice sounded strained; her fingers fumbled over the keys, striking wrong notes. Midway through the song she stopped and apologized. Halvard walked over to the piano and insisted she try again.

"Just pretend we're not here." He leaned forward so that his face nearly touched hers. She laughed nervously. I had never seen her so agitated.

The second time through, she found her voice, capturing the feeling of rapture that usually filled her at the piano. When she finished, Halvard was silent a moment, as though listening to the song's echo, then he asked if she would play another.

"Hunter could have played better," she declared ruefully. "I'm not used to performing, except before Nathan and Uncle Ray, and they never pay any attention."

"Anytime you want an audience, come play for us," Halvard offered.

Kitty returned to the sofa and tried to hide her embarrassment behind a teacup, her cheeks red, her eyes ablaze.

Not long after, Lisa spoke her first words, addressing her brother. "I think we ought to be heading home."

"No, please stay," Kitty insisted. "It's so rare we have company."

"I've got to be looking in on Trudy," Lisa added, looking at Kitty for the first time.

"Of course you do," Kitty allowed, regaining her composure. "Nathan, their coats."

As we left the house, Pa glanced up from his work a moment but did not return Halvard's wave.

"Please forgive my uncle," Kitty said.

"Don't apologize," Halvard replied. "We understand how he feels. It must be very difficult." Kitty met his eyes a moment. "A week from Sunday at two?"

"At two," Kitty repeated, watching them drive away.

CHAPTER

9

⟨❧⟩ Pa seemed particularly out of sorts that evening, pushing his half-eaten supper away in disgust, complaining he was "sick to death" of mutton. "It's bad enough having to wallow in sheep all day without eating it morning, noon, and night. What else is there?"

"A cellar full of vegetables," Kitty answered.

"What's happened to all the venison?"

"You ate it."

"Why the hell didn't you tell me?"

Kitty's eyes narrowed. They argued often about the killing of deer. She thought it cruel, especially since they seemed to treat the farm as a sort of sanctuary, often feeding at the edge of the pasture at twilight. To kill them was to betray a trust, she said. Pa scoffed at the idea, saying there were too many of them and not enough browse to go around in winter. "We're doing the herd a favor." That usually aroused an equivalent smirk from Kitty, who told him to explain the favor to the dead deer.

But this time she held her peace until Pa turned to me and said, "It's time you learned how to handle a rifle."

"Uncle Ray, he's too young."

"Hell he is! I wasn't more than seven or eight the first time my brothers took me hunting. Time he learned to take care of himself. A tree could fall on me tomorrow, for all I know. He ought to know how to put food on the table."

"He's only twelve."

"Tomorrow, after your lesson," he said, ignoring her.

"You're just going to walk up there and shoot one of those trusting deer?"

"If they're fool enough to let us, hell yes."

All the next morning my stomach fluttered at the thought of the hunt, imagining how proud Pa would be if I actually shot a deer, how angry if I missed. After Kitty finished going over my arithmetic, I ran up to the barn. Pa was in the tack room cleaning his rifle. The bolt lay on the workbench as he rammed an oiled cloth through the breech, withdrawing it black with grime.

"Your brother forgot to clean it," he grumbled. "You want a rifle to take care of you, you better learn to take care of it. You use it, you clean it."

He handed me the cleaning rod and watched as I reamed the barrel, then showed me how to replace the bolt. When the rifle was reassembled, we took it out behind the barn where a hand-drawn target hung on a distant tree. Pa removed a cartridge from his coat pocket and slipped it into the chamber, lay the rifle upon a fence rail, sighted carefully along the barrel, and fired. The bullet struck high and to the left of center. He adjusted the sight, reloaded, and this time drilled a hole in the middle of the smallest circle.

"Take your time," he said, handing me the rifle. "A good hunter is a patient hunter. Never pull the trigger, squeeze it. Hold your breath, make yourself so still you can feel the blood pulsing in your fingertips. Picture exactly where you want the bullet to go, then put it there with stillness and control."

I lay the rifle on the middle rail, closed one eye and sighted to the center of the target, held my breath until the blood pounded in my ears, and slowly squeezed the trigger. When the rifle clicked, Pa handed me a cartridge and quipped, "It works much better with this." I loaded the rifle and drew a deep breath. The barrel seemed to dance in rhythm with my heart, bobbing up and down. I waited for my hands to steady.

"You don't have forever, son. Wait too long and you've lost your quarry."

I pulled the trigger. The stock kicked back against my shoulder. A small piece of bark flew into the air. "At least you hit the tree," Pa said, squinting at the target. "Try again."

He handed me another cartridge, watching my hands as they opened and shut the heavy bolt. I liked the feel of it, the cold, steel ball in the center of my palm, the tightness of metal within metal sliding smoothly over oil.

"Squeeze," Pa reminded me, "don't jerk." I stiffened at the expectation of another painful blow to my shoulder. The shell exploded, more backward than forward, it seemed, shredding the lower left corner of the target.

"Better," Pa said. "Hold your breath this time."

Once more I loaded and fired, hitting the outermost ring. I turned to Pa with a smile, but he simply handed me another cartridge and said, "If you can't put it in either of the two inner circles, you'll never drop your game. Concentrate."

I fired five more shots, but each one drifted farther from the center, the last two missing the tree entirely. My shoulder throbbed. Pa kept reminding me to "squeeze," his voice growing colder and harder with each shot. Finally he grabbed the rifle, threw a cartridge into the breech, and said, "Watch me," exaggerating every movement as he described it. "Use your left hand more. Jam the rifle back against your shoulder. Tuck your right arm in against your ribs. Cock your head over the stock. Take a deep breath . . . then squeeeeeeze." His index finger moved backward imperceptibly until the gun exploded, blowing the center of the target apart.

I tried again but only succeeded in nipping a corner of the paper. Pa pursed his lips, then handed me the rest of the cartridges and said, "Don't come in until you've scored inside the second ring twice in a row."

As soon as he left, my hand grew steady. After half an hour nothing remained of the inner circle. My right shoulder ached, but success made the pain bearable. When I showed Pa the target he said, "Better," then rubbed my shoulder adding, "You'll get used to it."

We ate supper shortly after sunset, Pa in a better mood than he'd been in weeks, cheered by the thought of the hunt. Kitty used the occasion to mention the Hejdlings' invitation, hoping to persuade Pa to join us. At the mention of our neighbors, his good humor vanished.

"We don't have time for that nonsense. There's too much work to do," he grumbled.

"We could all use a little time off."

"Time off? There's no time off in this business, unless you're rich enough to pay others to do your work for you. I've never known a family of farmers with such clean hands." He scowled in the direction of the Hejdlings' farm.

"You'll even turn proper hygiene into cause for nastiness, won't you?" Kitty complained.

Pa grunted.

"Making social calls is not wasting time, Uncle

Ray, especially with your nearest neighbors. You can't live like a hermit."

"I'll live how I choose."

"They're doing us a big favor."

"They're not doing *me* a favor," he snapped. "I didn't ask them to take in Eric. If they don't want him, they can damn well send him packing. We're not forcing him on them."

"That's not the point," Kitty said. "They're just being neighborly."

"Then they should mind their own business. If Hejdling wants to throw away his money on foolishness, that's his business, but I'm not about to waste my time standing around jawing. Sunday's just another workday."

Rebel nosed open Kitty's door and ran into the kitchen.

"Didn't I tell you, no animals in the house?" Pa snapped, kicking the lamb away as it sniffed his boots.

"Uncle Ray, don't! He's been inside for weeks."

"Well, it's time he got back outside where he belongs."

Kitty waited for him to simmer down, then as he sat drinking his coffee she mentioned the party again, this time as an opportunity for Pa to speak to Eric.

"If he's got anything to say, he knows where to find me."

"Won't you meet him halfway?" she asked.

"No!"

"Will you never admit when you're wrong?"

"When I am, I will."

"You drove Eric out."

"He had a choice and he made it. You don't work, you don't eat. I warned Hejdling not to expect an honest day's labor from him."

"You're wrong, Uncle Ray. Halvard said he's never seen a harder worker."

Pa laughed bitterly. "What do they know about hard work over there?"

"You're not the only one in Providence who gets up before dawn."

"I don't have a houseful of children to help me, either."

"You would if you didn't drive them away."

Pa didn't reply. Kitty softened her voice. "Halvard said his father specifically asked that you join them. It's going to be a lovely celebration in honor of their new baby."

"Why all this sudden interest in Halvard?"

Kitty blushed.

"Don't be a fool, Kitty. You're thirty-one years old; he's barely out of diapers."

"Uncle Ray, please."

"He's nothing but a preening peacock, just like his father. What the hell do they have to feel so smug about, with that idiot boy running loose?"

"Bittle is not an idiot."

"They'll have to take care of him till the day he dies." Pa snorted bitterly. "That's what they want you for, Kitty, to be his nursemaid. Hejd-ling's a shrewd one. With all that time on his hands, he sits around thinking up ways to take advantage of the rest of us. They're not satisfied having stolen Eric, now they want you as well. Why don't you both go? Take the sheep while you're at it. Horses, too." He gripped the table with both hands. "You'll be a laughingstock."

In a voice subdued by pain, Kitty replied, "I am sick to death of your hatefulness," and left the kitchen, her eyes brimming with tears.

"What do you know about this?" Pa asked me.

"Nothing."

"You didn't notice anything when you went calling?"

"Nope."

He leaned forward over the table and took hold of my wrist. "Has that little runt been root-ing around here after dark, seeing Kitty behind my back?"

"I never saw him here but yesterday."

"You ever seen Kitty slip away?"

I shook my head.

"I ever catch that little weasel here uninvited, he'll leave with a seat full of buckshot. I'm gonna put a stop to this nonsense before the whole town's laughing at us." He addressed Kitty's closed door. "You want to make a fool of yourself, that's your business, but not while you're living under my roof! I don't want to see that whelp on my farm, you understand? I catch him sniffing around here again, I'll kick his hide all the way back to their 'ee-lectric' barn. He can save his fancy airs and his 'how do you dos' for someone who doesn't see right through him."

He turned back to the table and pushed his coffee away, spilling half of it on the table. "Get your jacket on, son. We got a buck to bag."

Only a faint trace of dark blue light remained in the western sky as we crossed the pasture. The mares huddled together for warmth, snorting in the cold; the colts lay curled at their feet. I kept my eyes focused on the woods, scanning the surface of the snow for any sign of movement, fearing the return of the mountain lion.

"You count the sheep tonight?" Pa asked.

"They're all in."

He draped the heavy rifle over my forearm. "Never walk with a loaded gun unless you've got your game in sight," he instructed. "You ready?"

"I think so."

"Don't tell me you think so. Yes or no?"

"Yes, sir."

"This is your hunt. No kill, no meat. We're all counting on you. One day you're gonna have a family of little ones to feed. It's time you learned how."

We followed the trail up to the top of the ridge, my heart beating in my ears. The old cabin loomed in the darkness. Beyond it the land leveled off.

"They've come this way," Pa said, pointing to fresh deer prints in the snow. "The wind's against us. That's good." A slight breeze blew across the ridge, rustling the pine needles. I walked alongside Pa until he remembered this was supposed to be my hunt and sent me on ahead, offering a steady stream of advice.

"They'll hear us long before we're in range, so you've got to lie in wait. Pick a part of the woods they're likely to cross. They need water and forage. Look for tracks, for places where they seem to gather, then settle yourself downwind with clear sighting and good support for your rifle. Get comfortable—it could take hours. And be still. One wrong move and they'll bolt."

We entered a stand of hemlock that led down a steep ravine to a swampy basin. Cranberries grew in the center of the bog, raspberries and huckleberries on the fringe. Pa said that when the snow was high, the deer fed on the raspberry canes.

"Find yourself a good blind," he said, buttoning my jacket up to my neck and pulling my hat down low over my ears. "This is it."

Near the bottom of the ravine I settled on a stump between two large pines and lay the rifle over a low branch. Pa hung back behind a wide spruce and watched me. After several minutes he pulled a plug of chewing tobacco from his pocket, leaned back against the tree, and blended into the night.

A warm thrill ran through me. I was on my own. I studied the marsh, trying to pierce the darkness of the opposite bank, mistaking every faint rustling for the approach of game. Minutes passed, my feet grew cold, my fingers numb. I looked back to see if Pa was still there, then I began to drift off, my mind wandering to warm rooms and hot baths, soft beds and the sound of Kitty singing.

When the cracking of twigs aroused me from my dreams, I nearly knocked the rifle from its perch. Across the bog a large buck emerged from the trees, his broad antlers catching in the low branches. He stepped forward cautiously, reluctantly leaving the cover of the pines, pausing with his nose in the air, sniffing, listening, then proceeding slowly toward the canes. I looked back at Pa. He nodded slowly. This was my chance. My heart began to flutter. *Aim for the chest,* I told myself. *Hold your breath, take your time, squeeze don't pull.* I pressed the rifle against my sore shoulder, laying my cheek alongside the stock. The buck stepped toward me, growing more distinct. *Steady,* I thought. *Wait until he turns sideways.*

At the raspberry canes he dropped his head, gradually presenting his chest to me as he fed. I held my breath, leaned into the stock, and slowly pulled the trigger. The rifle clicked—only clicked. I had forgotten to load it again! The buck's head shot up, his ears spread wide. I was afraid to look over my shoulder at Pa. I could feel him scowling at me.

The buck turned to stone, standing motionless for a minute or more, then snorted and resumed feeding. I carefully opened the bolt and inserted a cartridge, but the buck heard the breech click shut and leapt for the woods. When I turned toward Pa, he motioned angrily for me to remain where I was, pointing across the pond, then raising his fingers above his head like antlers. The buck stood just inside the trees.

I leaned over my rifle, watching him through the sight, praying for him to return and grant me another chance. But the buck was too wary. My eyes grew heavy, my feet began to tingle with numbness. When I looked back at Pa, he motioned for me to keep my eyes forward and remain still. I dozed off. Then suddenly the rifle fell from my hands, discharging as it hit the ground. The explosion seemed deafening in the stillness. When I looked up the buck was gone.

"What the hell was that!" Pa exploded, coming from behind his tree.

"I'm sorry," I whispered, unable to look him in the eye.

He yanked the rifle from my hands and opened the bolt, discharging the empty cartridge into his hand. "Maybe your cousin's right. You aren't ready for this. Though God knows when you'll ever be." He turned and climbed out of the ravine.

"I can do it," I insisted, running after him, tears clogging my throat.

"First you forget to load the damn thing, then you can't even stay awake long enough to get a shot off."

"I'm sorry."

"A lot of good that does when your family's starving."

"I'll try again tomorrow night."

"I don't think so."

"Please, Pa. I can do it."

He strode away, the gun resting on his forearm, his hands deep in his pockets.

Part Two

CHAPTER

10

A week later Kitty took me aside as I came in from late milking and whispered that a stranger was in the parlor talking to Pa. "He's been here an hour already," she said with interest. "Very tall man with a badly pocked face. Do you know him?"

I didn't think so.

"I overheard him mention something about your mother."

"Mama!" I cried, suddenly full of renewed hope. "I knew she wasn't dead!"

"Now, Nathan—"

Before she could finish I ran to the parlor, where I found the stranger sitting with his back to the door. He wore a long cowhide coat, denim trousers, and pointed boots with thick heels. A cloth bag and broad-brimmed hat lay beside his chair.

"Come say hello to your uncle," Pa said flatly, motioning me into the room. The stranger turned and smiled, revealing Mama's hazel eyes and a rugged, weather-beaten face capped by bushy brown hair. I judged him to be about Kitty's age.

"Is this Eric?" he asked.

"Nathan," Pa corrected.

"Baby Nate! Good God!" He grabbed my hand and pulled me toward him. His scarred face was full of warmth. "Don't you look the picture of your mother, God rest her soul."

My heart sank.

"Do you remember your uncle Zeke?" Pa asked coldly.

"How could he?" Zeke replied, fixing his bright eyes on me. "The last time I saw you, you were nothing but a tiny bundle of colic, causing your mama no end of worry."

"Sit," Pa ordered. I settled on the sofa. Zeke studied my face, shaking his head with a sad smile.

"Uncle Zeke's your mother's younger brother," Pa explained.

I remembered the name from letters Mama used to read us. She always referred to him as her "little brother" though he was more than a foot taller. In one letter he told us that the girl he was supposed to marry had disappeared the day before the wedding. Rather than feel sorry for himself, he had made his search for her sound so funny that we laughed over it.

"Did you ever get married?" I asked, reminding him of the letter.

Zeke chuckled. "You remember that, do you? I'm still on the lookout for that lass."

"Is that why you're here?"

"No, not exactly. It's a long story."

"Your uncle is going to stay with us awhile," Pa said without enthusiasm.

"I thought I might try my hand at sheep farming," Zeke explained. "And don't call me Uncle—it makes me feel like I'm too old to start over again. I hope you'll be patient with me. I've got a lot of learning to do."

Kitty entered the parlor bearing a tray, her face full of curiosity. "My niece Katherine," Pa said. Zeke turned toward her, then rose, towering over Kitty.

"All the Katherines I've ever known were saints," he said with a slight bow of his head.

"Just plain Kitty," she replied, her eyes laughing.

"Zeke will be joining us for supper," Pa told her.

"I hope you like mutton," she said, shooting a sly look across the room at Pa.

"After all the dust I've eaten on the road, anything prepared by your hands would be welcome."

Pa snorted, then told me to show Zeke upstairs, saying, "He'll sleep in Eric's bed."

Over supper Zeke told us about his years in Wyoming, the dream of ranching on the open plains that drew him there and the drought that left his ruined ranch in the hands of the banks. "When your pa sent me the sad news about my sister, I was too entangled to come east. But now it's all gone smash, so there's nothing left to keep me from visiting my nephews and telling them just how sorry I am. I know how much you must miss her. She was very special."

The room grew quiet a moment. There was so much he didn't know about Pa's temper and Eric's stubbornness and Mama running off.

"Are you sorry you went out west?" Kitty asked, refilling his plate.

"If someone staked me, I'd probably be fool enough to run right back and try it again," he admitted through a mouthful of potatoes. "But ranching will never be the same out there. The land just seemed to dry up and blow away these past few years. It hasn't rained for five years now. I've seen a whole lot of good men go under."

"No rain at all?" I asked.

"Not enough to keep the dust down. Winters were hard enough. You never saw so much snow, completely buried the cattle one year. But after the spring thaw, not another cloud except what the wind stirred up out of the earth. Some days you couldn't breathe without a handkerchief over your mouth, the dust was so thick."

"How could you bear it?" Kitty reflected.

"It's so beautiful. The mountains . . . you've

got to see them. In Jackson they shoot straight up from the plain like heaven's own gates. You live with them long enough, they enter your blood. I took strength from those rocks. I'd go back again, just to breathe that sharp, sobering air. Nothing like it anywhere in the country."

"Did you see any mountain lions?" I asked.

"Mountain lions, grizzlies, black bears, coyotes, wolves, moose, caribou, elk, deer, bison—you name it, we got it."

"We saw a mountain lion here a few weeks ago," I said.

"Did you really? They don't usually care for the scent of man. Must have been awful hungry."

"Killed a lambing ewe," Pa said.

"We had a pretty high bounty on them for a while," Zeke recalled. "They were taking down cattle during the heaviest snows. They can lay ambush in a stand of alder not ten feet from you, quiet as frost."

After supper we showed Zeke around the farm. The sheep were just beginning to return from the upper pasture, their bells clanging. I counted them as they entered the barn, then pushed in among them and counted again, my heart beginning to pound. "One's missing," I shouted to Pa over their hungry bleats.

"You sure?" he asked, his eyes already scanning the flock, tallying them up.

"I counted twice."

"Damn," he muttered, grabbing rifle and cartridges and hurrying out to the pasture.

"Is that your only rifle?" Zeke asked, following alongside.

Pa nodded.

"Times like this a shotgun comes in mighty handy."

Pa kept on walking, squinting through the twilight. Halfway up the pasture he broke into a loping run, feeding a cartridge into the breech.

"There he is," I shouted. The cat's phosphorescent eyes gleamed brightly as it lifted its blood-stained face from behind a dead ram. Pa stopped abruptly, shouldered the rifle, and fired. The huge cat leapt for the trees, arcing through the darkness like a black rainbow.

"You clipped it," Zeke shouted.

"Damn," Pa spat.

"I'll finish it off."

"Never mind."

"You don't want a wounded cat roaming around the farm," Zeke said, following Pa up the hill toward the bloody hump in the snow. "They're too unpredictable. Had one once come right down into the barn. They can get crazed when they're hit."

The ram had been killed exactly like the ewe, its throat and belly torn open.

"Look there, what did I tell you?" Zeke said,

pointing to blood-spotted snow several yards away.

Zeke continued toward the woods. "It's heavier here," he called through the darkness. "You definitely winged it, Ray. Good shot."

"Not good enough."

"I'll finish it off," he said, returning for the rifle.

"You'll never find him now."

"I've tracked in far worse conditions."

"Let him, Pa," I pleaded, wishing we were rid of it.

"The cat's not far," Zeke said, cocking his ear toward the trees.

"How can you tell?" I asked.

"After a while you just get a sixth sense about anything that preys on your livestock. It's still out there, watching us, licking its wound. It might retreat or it might go on the attack. You never know. You don't want to chance it, Ray."

Reluctantly Pa handed him the rifle. Zeke loaded and shouldered it, sighting along the barrel. Then he walked noiselessly into the woods. Pa took hold of the ram's hind legs and began dragging him back to the barn. Halfway there a rifle shot shattered the brittle silence.

"You think he got him?" I asked anxiously.

"If he's more comfortable with a shotgun than a rifle, odds are he missed."

I hoped Pa was wrong. "Do you mind Uncle Zeke staying with us?"

"Not if he does his share. We can use an extra pair of hands."

"Is he gonna stay long?"

"That all depends if he's gotten over his failure or brought it with him."

"What do you mean?"

"Fetch the lamp."

Pa hung the ram on the hook outside the barn and began to skin it, stopping occasionally to blow on his frozen fingers. As Pa worked, Zeke's lanky figure moved down through the pasture with long strides. As the lamplight touched his face, Zeke screwed up his mouth in an expression of disappointment. "Couldn't get a clear shot."

Pa snorted but said nothing.

Late the next afternoon Pa told me to take Doc into the woods and haul out some freshly cut timber. Kitty didn't like me going alone. Even Zeke thought it unwise. But Pa insisted I had nothing to worry about. "After two bullets, if that cat has any sense at all, it's long gone."

"At least let him take the rifle," Zeke suggested.

Pa laughed bitterly. "All he's likely to do is shoot himself in the foot."

I entered the woods trembling. A sharp wind made the swaying trees groan. I kept looking over my shoulder, working fast, tossing the heavy logs onto the sled in a frenzied effort to get back home before dark.

As the light began to fade, Bianca appeared, settling on a branch above my head. I felt relieved. She cooed once, then headed back toward the pasture.

"Don't go," I called.

To my surprise she returned, circled my head, and flew off again.

I turned to pick up another log, then froze. Something was moving through the snow. My skin bristled. A branch moved. I looked for shelter, a stick, anything to protect myself. Then Rebel bounded toward me, his black fur a blur in the deepening darkness.

"You scared me half to death," I said, picking him up. He shivered in my hands. "Where's the rest of the flock?"

Bianca flew across our path once more, nearly hitting me with her wings.

"Stop that!" I cried.

When I turned back to the woodpile, a distant boulder suddenly sprouted eyes. Rebel grew rigid as the dark silhouette of the mountain lion rose up from the rock, snarling. In an instant the huge cat compressed itself and exploded toward my face. A scream rose to my lips; my arms shot forward. I felt the concussion of a rifle shot. The airborne cat shuddered as though deflected by a huge hand, hitting me in the chest instead of the face, knocking me backward against a tree.

For a moment I neither saw nor heard. My eyes went black, my ears filled with the thumping of my own blood. A voice shouted, "Nate, you all right?" Footsteps tramped through the snow. Somewhere Rebel bleated, but I could not get my eyes to clear. I felt something hot on my cheek, reached up, then held my gloved hand to my eyes. I was bleeding. The news reached me from a great distance. I hardly knew what it meant. I felt like sleeping, wanting nothing more than to lie back and close my eyes.

Zeke knelt beside me, pressing a handful of snow to my face. The sting revived me. "Hold that there," he said, replacing his hand with mine. Using the rifle barrel he prodded the dead mountain lion at my feet.

"That's one big cat," he observed. Bianca returned, perching just above my head.

"Rebel," I muttered. My lips and tongue moved with difficulty. "Where's Rebel?"

A faint cry issued from somewhere near the mountain lion. Zeke grabbed the cat by its front legs and flipped it over. Rebel lay buried in the snow, dazed but unharmed.

"You okay, little guy?" Zeke asked, scooping him up and brushing the snow from his coat. Rebel bleated indignantly, demanding to be set down.

"Feisty little devil," Zeke said, releasing him. Rebel approached the dead cat and sniffed the bloody snow beside its face.

"Get away from there," Zeke said, pushing Rebel toward me with his boot. "How's that cheek feel?" It had grown numb from the snow.

"What happened?" I muttered, my throat raw.

"You were about that close to becoming supper," he said, holding his thumb and forefinger a few inches apart. He helped me to my feet. I studied the dead mountain lion. Blood had congealed beside the ragged bullet wound in her neck. Her coat also revealed an older shoulder wound.

"That's where your father winged her," he said. "A beauty, isn't she?"

Before I could respond, my stomach stiffened and I knelt down in the snow and retched.

CHAPTER
11

❧ I never heard Pa admit he was wrong about the mountain lion or thank Zeke for saving my life, but after we brought the big cat in on the sled, Pa seemed to hold him in less contempt than he had the night Zeke missed his shot. In his own wordless way, he was pleased to have Zeke around. The two of them began taking on chores Pa had been meaning to attend to for months, like repairing broken windows and fixing leaky roofs.

The following Sunday, Zeke and I were standing on adjacent ladders nailing new siding against the barn when Kitty called from the kitchen, "Wash up, boys, and get changed. We're due at the Hejdlings' in half an hour."

"You joining us, Ray?" Zeke called through a chink in the wall. Pa shook his head without looking up, straining against a bent nail in Doc's horseshoe.

"Any message for Eric?"

Pa glared up at him a minute before returning to the difficult nail. Zeke looked at me with raised eyebrows, then nodded toward the house. I climbed down and returned the tools to the tack room while he carried the ladders to the back of the barn, stopping at Doc's stall on the way out.

"Sure you won't join us?"

Pa yanked the old shoe off with a grunt and tossed it into the dirt.

"Ought to let yourself have a little relaxation now and again," Zeke suggested.

"Spare me your sermons."

"No sermon. Just wish you'd go a little easy on yourself, take a break, have some fun."

"Watching Hejdling strut around like a prize cock is not my notion of fun. Go, if you like. I've got shoeing to finish."

"It would mean a lot to Eric."

"You don't know the first thing about Eric," Pa snapped.

"Maybe I don't, but I know this: I lost ten years of my life out west, encountered my share of disappointment and misery, but I never gave in to the kind of bitterness and anger that rules your days."

Pa kept on working. Zeke shook his head and left the barn, followed by Bianca, who leapt from a rafter and settled on his right shoulder. Zeke smiled at her, then clapped me on the back and said, "We'll just have to do your pa's celebrating for him."

By the time we arrived, the Hejdlings' driveway was crowded with sleighs and wagons and even two fancy motorcars, their narrow, spoked wheels wrapped in chains. The front door stood open, guests passing in and out, some bearing presents, others holding glasses of punch. Kitty smoothed her brown woolen skirt, then felt about her head for delinquent strands of hair. Her face shone with eagerness. Zeke had dug into his carpetbag and retrieved a fancy white shirt with silver buttons, pressed a pair of black pants, brushed out his cowhide jacket, and polished his cowboy boots.

Bittle bounded down the stairs as we pulled up to the front porch, taking hold of the horses and winking wordlessly at me. His father met us at the door, dressed in a dark gray suit, his white hair brushed and gleaming. He took Kitty's hand and introduced himself to Zeke.

"I understand you're quite a marksman."

"A lucky one," Zeke replied modestly.

"You bear a striking resemblance to your late sister."

"She would not have appreciated the comparison." Zeke smiled, rubbing his weathered face.

"She was a fine woman," Mr. Hejdling mused. "Please accept my condolences." As he spoke, his eyes focused on a carriage just pulling up to the porch. "Please make yourselves at home," he said, moving quickly past us.

We crossed the front hall to the dining room, Zeke blinking in astonishment at the opulence. All the chairs had been pushed against the walls, the carpet rolled up. The center of the room was occupied by a long table crowded with platters of food, a huge bouquet of flowers, and an enormous bowl filled with frothy pink punch and a heavy block of ice. A continuous stream of guests circled the table, refilling their plates and cups, talking loudly. The women occupied the chairs along the wall, balancing dishes on their laps; the men stood together in small groups near the table; the children sat cross-legged on the floor.

"There's the baby!" Kitty shouted over the din, pointing through the parlor doors. Trudy sat beside the fireplace, looking tired but happy as she rocked a small cradle at her feet. Gregory stood beside her, his clean-shaven face shining with pleasure at the attention his newborn son was getting. Beside the cradle lay a pile of neatly wrapped packages.

Kitty worked her way through the crowd, dropping to her knees to admire the sleeping boy. "He's so beautiful," she whispered, looking up at Trudy, who smiled in speechless gratitude, her tired eyes expressing both worry and adoration. Kitty presented our gift. "My mother put me to sleep on a lambskin just like this for the first six months of my life, and she swears I never kept her up a single night."

"God bless you," Trudy moaned.

Kitty took the empty chair beside her, staring longingly at the baby while Zeke and I returned to the dining room. When we could squeeze nothing more on our plates, Zeke dipped a cup into the nearly empty punch bowl, took a sip, and declared in disbelief, "Champagne! No wonder everyone's so jolly." He drained his cup and quickly refilled it, his eyes radiating pleasure.

As we stood eating in a corner of the noisy room, Halvard entered bearing two large bottles and a heavy silver pitcher. He carefully unwrapped the champagne and popped the corks, letting it foam over into the punch bowl. Then he added the contents of the silver pitcher and declared the punch "fully restored." Bittle squeezed between a knot of guests when his brother's back was turned, quickly filled his own glass, and returned to his post by the front door. Halvard worked his way through the crowd to greet Zeke, shouting over the din, "Kitty tells me you've just returned from Wyoming." The two of them couldn't have been more opposite in appearance. Before they could strike up a conversation, a sea of faces pressed between them and Halvard was borne away.

We emptied our plates, then squeezed our way out to the front hall.

"No sign of Eric," Zeke observed, looking toward the kitchen.

Mr. Hejdling emerged from his den, carrying an open box of cigars. "Enjoying yourselves, boys?" he asked, offering Zeke a cigar.

"Long time since I tasted such fine champagne," Zeke replied, accepting the cigar. He seemed as comfortable around strangers as among family.

"I'm sorry your brother-in-law was not able to join us."

"He's still in mourning," Zeke explained.

"I understand," Mr. Hejdling said, squeezing my shoulder before slipping into the dining room to distribute his cigars.

"Nice fellah," Zeke observed.

Sonja emerged from the kitchen carrying a basket of hot rolls.

"Have you seen my nephew Eric?" Zeke asked.

"No," she said, barely giving us a look.

"Bobcat, that one," Zeke observed with a smile, watching her enter the dining room.

"Her sister's worse," I replied.

"Have I met her yet?"

I scanned the dining room, then shook my head. Zeke headed for the front porch, where we found Bittle sitting on the steps, his mouth stuffed with food.

"You seen Eric?" I asked. He pointed with his chin toward the barn. Zeke set off down the slippery driveway, lost his balance, and slid most of the way on his rump, whooping and laughing. I followed cautiously behind.

"Haven't done that in years." He grinned through glassy eyes while brushing himself off.

The double doors to the barn stood open at both ends, sunlight glinting off the wet concrete floor. Zeke whistled in admiration as he walked down the center, his head turning left and right and left again, taking in the spotless stalls, the scrubbed and shining milking pails, the butter churns and ice freezers, the freshly washed windows. The ceiling was hung with electric lights spaced along a black wire running the length of the barn. Where ours was dark, dirty, and drafty, theirs was light and clean and as well insulated as their house. "They run a tight ship," he observed. "Never seen such a spanking barn. You could eat off the floor."

At the far end we squinted into the sunlight, scanning the white hillside for Eric. The herd stood huddled beneath a barren oak tree, pulling at several large bales of hay. The calves wandered in and out of a small grain crib. We plodded uphill, calling Eric's name, climbing over fences, the warm sun pocking the surface of the snow. Zeke pushed back his hat and unzipped his leather jacket, then turned and looked across the valley at our farm. A solitary black figure moved across the high pasture.

"There's your pa," he said.

I had forgotten to hay the colts, I realized, watching Pa heave forkfuls into the snow.

"I wanted to be like your pa once," Zeke reflected, leaning against a fence rail. "He didn't use to be so sullen. Whenever disaster threatened out west, I asked myself, 'What would Ray do? He'd know how to handle this.' But he's changed. I guess we all have." He scooped up a ball of wet snow and hurled it at my chest. "And you've changed the most." I returned fire.

A voice from the kitchen called shrilly for Eric. Lisa stood on the back step, a white shawl draped over her shoulders.

"That Lisa?" Zeke asked. When I nodded, he hurried up to the kitchen to introduce himself.

"Beautiful place you've got here," he said, tipping his hat. "I'm Zeke, Eric's uncle."

"Have you seen him?" Lisa replied coldly, her eyes searching the fields.

"We thought maybe you could tell us."

"We need him in the kitchen," she said brusquely, then stepped back inside.

When we returned to the parlor, Halvard was trying to coax Kitty to the piano.

"Hal told me what a lovely voice you have," Trudy said. Ethan lay bellowing in her arms.

"She certainly does," Halvard insisted.

"I'm so out of practice," Kitty said, blushing.

"You're among friends," he declared, pulling her toward the piano. Her hair had come partially undone, red coils springing off in all directions. "Play that lullaby you sang for us."

Kitty sat at the piano and played a scale. "I'm really not—"

"Play!" Halvard ordered, smiling. The sound of the notes had silenced Ethan. "You see, he loves it."

Kitty began the lullaby. Ethan listened, his eyes fixed on the ceiling, his lips puckered into a small O. By the end, he had fallen asleep.

"That was lovely," Trudy whispered. Halvard beamed.

During the song, Zeke had slipped back to the dining room. He helped himself to another glass of punch and a large red apple, then suggested we continue our search for Eric. Sonja pointed us toward the back steps leading to his attic room. We climbed the stairway and knocked on the door. When no one answered, we entered the small room. It was bare except for a narrow bed and dresser. A single dormer window faced our farm. The bed had been stripped, the drawers emptied. I lifted the counterpane and pillow, discovering a note written in Eric's hand: "I've only taken what I came with," it said. "I won't be back."

"Looks like our boy's run off again," Zeke declared.

CHAPTER

12

❧ The third week in March a blizzard dumped more than a foot of wet snow over the valley, dressing the broad hemlock branches in thick white skirts, bending the birches to the ground. All the ragged contours of the farm were softened, stone walls becoming little more than ripples on a vast white sea. At times the flakes fell so thick and fast that the woodpile outside the kitchen door disappeared. Daylight itself barely filtered through the thick storm. In the unnatural darkness I slept an hour longer than usual, huddling beneath warm covers while the wind howled through cracks in the windows. It seemed as though winter would never end, that the snow would continue to fall until everything was buried but the spiny tops of the tallest white pines.

When I reached the kitchen, Kitty was just beginning to light the stove, her eyes heavy with sleep. Pa was already out, shoveling snow off the goat shed to keep the roof from collapsing. Zeke came in carrying firewood, his hair frosted white. Hunter opened one eye as if to ask why we were making such a commotion in the middle of the night. It was so dark, Kitty lit the kitchen lamp and kept it burning until noon, when the storm began to ease.

Zeke spent the better part of the morning sitting by the window, whittling long, narrow branches into short dowels, whistling tunelessly. After half an hour Kitty asked crossly, "Are you doing that just to annoy?"

"This?" he asked, holding up his knife.

"That infernal whistling."

"Sorry," he apologized, winking at me.

"I hope you intend on cleaning up that mess," Kitty said, pointing to the growing pile of shavings between his boots. She was in an unusually sour mood that morning, annoyed, it seemed, by so much new snow just as the calendar promised spring.

"Katerina," Zeke replied, "I not only intend to clean up this mess, I intend to sweeten your disposition as well."

"I'll settle for a clean floor. You want to sweeten someone, try Uncle Ray."

Zeke continued to whittle until he had cut about three dozen pegs, each half an inch in diameter and about six inches long. After sweeping up the shavings, he stuffed the pegs in his coat pockets and trudged through the high snow to the barn.

For an hour all was quiet while I did my morning lesson and Kitty kneaded dough, working sullenly. Pa came in, glanced around the quiet kitchen, then went out again. As the sky began to lighten, Zeke took to hammering something up in the barn.

"What in God's name is that man up to now?" Kitty complained, her forehead knotted with annoyance. Every hammer blow reverberated through the house. "Nate, go up there and tell him to stop that racket."

Zeke stood before the workbench, holding a sheet of tin roofing and a pair of shears. He was cutting and banging the metal into what he called hats, ovals with turned-under edges. A dozen lay heaped on the floor. Several wooden pegs stood upright in the vise, each with a small hole drilled lengthwise through the center. Around his feet he had gathered five milk pails and three water buckets.

"Almost ready," he declared. "Any other pails about?"

"What for?"

"We've got maple syrup to make."

"Now, in this storm?" I asked.

"Couldn't ask for better conditions. Can't you feel it warming? When you get a sudden thaw after a hard frost this time of year, the sap runs like the trees have sprung a leak."

We collected thirty pails in all, loaded them onto the sled along with an auger and a wooden mallet, and pulled it up to the north end of the pasture. When we reached the sugar maples, Zeke wiped the wet snow from the bark of one tree and put his ear to it.

"If you're real quiet, you can hear the sap running," he said.

I placed my ear against the craggy trunk.

"Listen hard," Zeke insisted, making the sound of galloping horses with his tongue. "Did you hear that?" He slapped me on the shoulder, took out the auger, and drilled a hole the width of his thumb through the soft bark, fitting it with one of his wooden spiles. After tapping it securely into place, he hung a bucket from it.

"Sap runs first in the warmest trees," he said, moving along the border of the woods and drilling into another maple. "How come your father never sugared? Shame to let it go to waste. Out west I dreamt of doing this every spring, but all we had were alder and lodgepole pine."

The sky gradually brightened. By midafternoon the sun broke through, pouring light over the bleached countryside. As we moved from tree to tree, huge clumps of snow slipped from high branches, hitting the ground with a dull thud. After drilling the last hole, we returned to the first tree and found the bucket a quarter full.

"See what I mean," Zeke said, sticking his finger under the spout. "It's running fast. Try it." It tasted just like water with a faint metallic flavor.

"It's a long way from being syrup," Zeke explained. "We have to boil it way down to get it sweet. It'll take all those buckets just to make one really good pailful."

I knew then why Pa had never bothered. I could hear him saying, "Any man who wastes that much effort just to sweeten his griddle cakes doesn't value his time."

We sat on the stone wall at the edge of the pasture, our coats open, watching the sunlight turn the white valley into water. "Your mama loved maple syrup. Used to help collect it every spring when we were little."

"We never had any here."

"I should have come back sooner and made you a batch. Sometimes that's all it takes to set things right."

Squirrels peeked from their knotholes and scrambled down the sides of trees, searching for food beneath the snow.

"Never seen the world look so clean," Zeke observed, his warm breath visible in the frosty air. "If this were my place, I'd homestead right here at the top of the pasture, the world at my doorstep, the woods at my back. I always imagined life started like this, not in some tropical garden but under snow, everything just as pure and white as it is now."

"I guess that's why Mama loved the cabin," I reflected.

"We had a lot in common."

"I dream of her all the time," I said.

"Like what?" he asked.

"Mostly that she's in the kitchen or out back tending her garden or hugging the sheep."

"Hugging the sheep?" Zeke laughed.

"Whenever we had to cull one, she'd throw her arms around its neck and ask its forgiveness."

"That was Maggie," Zeke said, shaking his head slowly. "Must have been hard on her, all those deaths."

"The fighting was worse."

"Guess so." He lay a hand on my shoulder.

"For a long time I thought she'd come back," I admitted, "but I don't anymore."

"I guess I came all this way for the same reason," he revealed. "I had to see with my own eyes that she was really gone. I couldn't imagine it."

Zeke turned his face to the sun.

"Do you like Halvard?" I asked. He'd been to the farm repeatedly since the party, sometimes sitting in the parlor with Kitty, sometimes taking her out for a drive.

"Seems nice enough."

"Pa doesn't care for him."

"That's no surprise. He doesn't want to lose Kitty."

"Are you ever gonna marry?" I asked.

"It's a complicated business, marriage. A man's got to have something to offer a woman in exchange for all her hard work and childbearing. I'm empty-handed at the moment."

"You work hard."

"That's not always enough."

"If you found someone you liked, would you marry her?"

"You got anyone in mind?"

"How about Kitty," I suggested.

Zeke chuckled. "She'd be a boon to any man, no question about it. She's got the energy of three women. But I'm afraid she's already spoken for, and even if she weren't, I'm in no position to offer her or anyone else a home. Halvard, on the other hand, faces nothing but glory."

The temperature continued to rise through the afternoon. Melting snow ran from the roof in a thousand tiny streams.

"Say good-bye to winter," Zeke said, stepping outside after supper. The air felt softer; gone was the harsh bite of frost. Kitty joined us, shaking out the tablecloth, then breathing deeply.

"Doesn't that feel wonderful," she whispered reverently, clutching the cloth to her chest. "I am so sick of winter."

"Aren't we all," Zeke reflected, watching Kitty pull the day's wash from the line and lay it over her shoulder. The leading edge of a rising moon appeared through the trees.

"Ray seems a whole lot mellower lately, doesn't he?" Zeke observed. Pa sat at his desk going over accounts.

"I'm worried about him," Kitty said, her voice just above a whisper.

"Seems fine to me," Zeke said.

"He got a letter yesterday."

"From Eric?" I asked.

"Don't know. He didn't leave it on the desk."

"Probably more wool orders," Zeke decided.

"I don't think so. After he opened it, he sat down hard, then stared into those pigeonholes until I asked if anything was wrong."

"What did he say?" I asked, wondering if it was about Mama.

"Nothing. I'm sure it was bad news. We haven't heard a word from Eric since he left. He could be lying in a gutter somewhere, for all we know."

"Don't you think Ray would have said something?"

"I can't tell with him anymore, can't even provoke him into an argument."

"Never thought I'd hear you complain about that."

"You know what I mean. He's just not himself."

"He's resting up," Zeke said. "We've got the hardest season ahead of us. He's saving his strength."

"I wish that was all."

"Stop worrying."

We lapsed into silence, watching the moon climb above the trees, casting silver shadows across the snow. The sheep banged against the inside of the barn as they bedded down for the night. Dart snorted and shook his mane as he ambled about the corral.

"Haven't seen much of Halvard lately," Zeke remarked, trying to draw Kitty out of her worry.

I expected a sharp response, but she just continued staring at the moon.

"I trust our young swain's in the pink," Zeke probed.

Still Kitty didn't answer. But in the darkness she shivered.

"We could take a drive over in the morning, see how little Ethan's doing," Zeke offered more softly, beginning to sense Kitty's pain. "I've got to pick up some supplies in town."

"He needs a younger woman," Kitty blurted out, shaking her head as she addressed the snow at her feet. "Everyone says so. They all smirk whenever they see me. I thought I could ignore it, but I can't."

"Why, Katherine Burns," Zeke said with exaggerated surprise, "I never thought I'd see the day you paid heed to gossiping tongues. You're tougher than that."

"I used to think so. But you can't survive without a community. Uncle Ray may try, he may say he doesn't care what they think, treat them with scorn even when they try to help him, but without townsfolk buying his wool and mutton, he'd have to sell the farm and hire himself out just like you and me. It's not pride that keeps him so independent, it's their willingness to let him be." She looked across the valley. "I think I could live with the whispers. My vanity got used to that long ago. But I couldn't bear their mocking him, too. He's a good man. He deserves better."

"You can't stop people from talking, Kitty, you know that, no matter how saintly you live your life. What difference does it make?"

"The difference between a happy marriage and one racked by doubts. Sooner or later all that poison will seep into our veins. If I thought they might one day accept me, I'd hang on and fight. But I know they won't. It goes too much against the grain. They don't want to see their own sons marrying old women like me, already set in their ways. They want submissive young daughters-in-law who'll do their bidding and bear a houseful of children."

"Is that what Halvard wants?" Zeke asked.

"I told him it's impossible."

"When?"

"Day before yesterday. It's just as well. Spring's coming. There's too much work to do. No time for all this courting foolishness."

"You sound just like Ray."

"Maybe this time he's right," Kitty said, stepping back into the house.

Zeke watched her go. "There's more to this than she's admitting," he said to me. "Could be young Halvard gave her the brush and she's too proud to admit it."

"Why's he been spending so much time with her if he wasn't going to marry her?" I asked.

"Just amusing himself, I guess. Not much else to do when the snow's so deep. But now spring's coming and the sap's starting to rise."

It didn't make sense to me, but then nothing did since Mama left.

"Falling in love never makes sense," Zeke said. "There ain't a person living or dead who didn't come to regret it sooner or later. But that's love. The only thing worse than failure is success."

13

A cold drizzle fell the next morning while Zeke and I collected the sap buckets and hauled them to the lean-to, where he'd built an evaporator to boil down the sap. Fog drifted across the valley. Large, tawny patches of grass began to appear as the snow receded. Throughout the day the rain grew stronger, turning the snow to slush, the earth to mud. By midafternoon, when Zeke and I rode into town for provisions, Providence Creek had overflowed its banks, raging past the commons, carrying fallen trees, backyard debris, and several drowned piglets.

On the way home we passed the mail truck sunk up to its axles in mud. We helped push it free, the spinning wheels spattering us from head to toe. Before we left, the postman handed us a letter addressed to Pa with a New York City postmark.

"It's from Eric," I said, recognizing his handwriting.

"That's a relief," Zeke replied.

"Can I open it?"

"Your pa won't be none too pleased."

"I gotta know how he is."

"It's your hide."

I wiped my hands on a dry corner of my jacket, then carefully unsealed it. "He's in New York," I told Zeke, "studying art!"

"Well, good for him. By all accounts, that's just where he oughtta be."

When we turned into our drive, Kitty approached without an umbrella or coat, her fiery curls matted against her forehead, her sweater and skirt drenched with rain.

"Will you look at the two of you!" She burst out laughing. "Is there an inch that isn't covered with mud?" She pulled me down from the wagon with wet hands and spun me around.

"The mail truck got stuck in the mud," I explained, then showed her the letter. "Eric's in New York."

She read it, then threw her head back and smiled, letting the rain wash over her face.

"You're soaking wet," I said.

"I guess I am," she said, twirling around. "It got so hot in the house, I had to come out and cool off." The rain dripped from her nose and chin.

"You ought to be cool enough by now," Zeke observed.

"Almost." She spun around again.

"What is it?" I asked.

"Nothing, nothing," she insisted, her eyes blazing.

"Tell us."

"No, I can't. It's too ridiculous."

"Is it Halvard?" Zeke asked.

She screamed, then pressed me to her chest. "Don't say another word, neither of you, nothing, not a sound."

I couldn't help but laugh, infected by her giddiness, happy that Eric was all right. She took my hand and pulled me along the drive, splashing through the deepest puddles like a child while Zeke drove up behind. By the time we reached the house, she was as mud-spattered as we were.

The three of us stepped inside the lean-to and watched the steam rise from the boiling sap. "It still has a ways to go," Zeke declared, dipping a long-handled spoon into the pan and offering us a taste, "but it's getting there." The syrup was still thin but very sweet. I passed the spoon to Kitty, but she shook her head, then burst out laughing.

"Is there something you'd like to tell us?" Zeke asked.

"Maybe . . . I don't know . . . yes . . . no, not now . . . soon."

"Her brain's definitely addled. Can only mean one thing."

"Hold your tongue, Ezekiel," Kitty insisted, running to the house.

We followed her, shedding our wet clothes by

the door, then stood in soggy drawers before the stove while Kitty disappeared inside her room.

"You get out of those wet things before you catch your death," she called from behind her closed door.

On my way to the stairs I found Pa sitting alone in the parlor, staring out at the rain, his right hand kneading his bad leg. I handed him Eric's letter. He read it without noticing it had been opened, then set it aside. He had something else on his mind.

"Soon as you both get changed I'd like to speak with you."

Zeke looked at me knowingly.

When we came down, Kitty was standing by the window, a towel wrapped around her head.

"Do you want to tell them or should I?" Pa began.

Kitty tried to speak, then shook her head, whispering, "I can't," tears running from her smiling eyes.

"Halvard has asked to marry her," Pa said dully, waving the mysterious letter from the day before.

"Well, good for him," Zeke declared. "Nice to know there's one man in this town with sense enough and good taste."

Kitty beamed at him, wiping her eyes on her sleeve. After what she had said the night before, I was too stunned to respond.

"Aren't you happy for me?" Kitty asked, taking my hands.

"I guess so. But yesterday—"

"You guess so?" Kitty asked, pretending to be hurt.

"I am. It's only—"

"Yesterday was yesterday," Zeke answered for her. "Time and a good night's sleep change things, don't they?"

"I was a goose," she said.

"When's the big day?" Zeke asked.

Kitty laughed in answer.

"June weddings are nice," he suggested.

"That's much too soon," she cried.

"What about *us?*" I asked. "Who'll do the cooking?"

Zeke spread out his arms and said, "You mean to tell me you've never tasted Uncle Zeke's mutton and maple syrup? They rave about it in Jackson."

"We'll manage just fine," Pa said brusquely. "We did so before."

Kitty frowned. "Who says I'm leaving?"

"You marry a man, you go live with him," Pa declared.

"Who says I'm marrying him?"

"Then what's all this idiot dancing and carrying on about?" Pa asked.

"I never had a choice like this to make, never thought I would," Kitty admitted. "I'm just enjoying it, that's all."

Pa frowned. Zeke laughed.

"Do you think I'd be this happy," she said, turning to me, "if I thought it meant I'd have to leave you? You're my family now, all of you. I can't make a decision like this alone."

"It's not our decision to make," Pa said.

"You wouldn't say that if I were your daughter."

"You're not my daughter, you're my niece, and old enough to know your own mind. I won't stand in your way, if that's what you're afraid of."

"I'm not afraid of anything, Uncle Ray, except hurting the ones I love."

"You know how I feel."

"That I'm too old," she shot back.

"I'm not saying you're too old to marry, just too old for a boy of twenty-two."

"And if Zeke wanted to marry Lisa, what would you say?"

"Hold on a minute," Zeke cried. "I've no intention of marrying that lynx or anyone else."

"But if he did," Kitty pursued, "would you feel the same way?"

"A man can marry whomever he likes."

"She's not even eighteen."

"That's just the way it is."

"It's not fair."

"Maybe not. There's a whole lot in this world that ain't fair."

"You make it sound as though I'm old enough

to be his mother. There's only eight years between us."

"Almost nine, and that's nine years too many. You're a woman, Kitty. It's different, that's all."

I held my tongue but agreed with Pa. People *were* smirking behind her back. Some called her "the spinster niece," others, "old Mother Hubbard." But Kitty had turned defiant.

"No, it's not different, Uncle Ray. It's exactly the same," she said calmly.

"Then you're the only one who sees it that way."

"Maybe so, but that doesn't make it any less true. You find yourself up against the whole town often enough without feeling the least inclination to change your mind."

"Not when they're all acting like fools."

Kitty lay her palms face up and smiled.

"You think I'm acting like a fool?" Pa asked, not with anger but curiosity.

She laughed. "I think there's hope for you, Uncle Ray."

It rained the whole week, pushing back the great white glacier that had held the countryside frozen for so many weeks, leaving a sodden brown landscape in its place. Water ran from every surface, dripped from every branch, found its way through every crack and seam in roof and wall. The earthen floor of the sheepcote turned to mud, etched by a dozen small streams. The straw bedding soaked up the water, growing heavy as stone. Roads became so impassable that nothing moved but the mail truck, which kept getting stuck.

Pa spent most of that week readying the cultivators and harrows for spring planting, and teaching me how to operate them. Zeke finished collecting and boiling down the sap, presenting us with eight gallons of maple syrup at week's end. "Gonna drown my mutton in this tonight," he declared with a wink.

As the rain tapered off, we spent a week replacing rotting boards in the hay wagon. By then Zeke knew all our winter routines and had even learned to card and spin wool, sitting at Kitty's elbow every evening, offering his hands whenever she needed someone to help wind the yarn. He was an eager student, enjoying nothing so much as a new challenge. In anticipation of spring planting, he began clearing away scrub, adding almost an acre to our cornfield.

When the rain finally stopped, the deeply rutted barnyard mud became as thick as cement, drying slowly under overcast skies. After three days, the sun finally broke through, pulling moisture from the ground and with it the first flowers of spring. Each morning dawned a little warmer. One afternoon I found Kitty hanging wash on the line, singing softly to herself. Mama's crocuses had just blossomed beside the vegetable garden. Two honeybees, the first of the season, hovered over the flowers.

"Doesn't that make you smile?" Kitty asked.

I shrugged. Ever since she had told us about Halvard's proposal, I didn't feel like smiling at anything. It was like losing Mama all over again.

"Are you feeling all right?" she asked, placing the back of her hand against my forehead. "You're not coming down with something, are you? You haven't been eating well lately."

"I'm okay," I said sullenly.

"It's Halvard, isn't it?"

I shook my head.

"You don't fool me for one minute. Now for the benefit of the mule-headed and the hard of hearing, let me repeat: Halvard is not going to take me away from you. Do you understand? I'm not going anywhere, not for a while. Halvard understands and accepts that. Why can't you?"

"Are you gonna marry him?"

"Not immediately. We've still got some wrinkles to iron out."

"But you will, one day, and then you'll leave us."

"Just you wait and see."

Zeke came down from the upper pasture, his forearms covered with grease. "Your pa wants you out back," he said, stepping into the barn for tools.

"Go," Kitty said. "And cheer up. Uncle Ray's got a surprise for you."

"What?"

"You'll see."

Zeke caught up to me at the pasture gate, carrying the heavy toolbox. "You're quiet today. Feel like talking?"

"Nope."

"Seems to run in the family. Haven't had two words out of your pa all morning. Kitty wasn't kidding when she said the English language would have died out up here long ago if it hadn't been for her. What's eating you both? Is it Kitty?"

I shrugged.

He scooped up a handful of new grass and sprinkled it over my head like wedding rice. "She deserves a little happiness, you know."

"I'd rather she married you than Halvard."

Zeke laughed. "You think your father's unhappy now? At least Halvard's got some substance to him."

"You've got substance."

"Mostly debts."

Pa lay beneath the manure spreader, trying to repair a slipped chain. Zeke handed him the toolbox. The bed of the spreader was heaped high with manure and straw. Pa banged away, grunting and swearing, then emerged from between the wheels, wiping his oil-stained hands on his overalls.

"You got it?" Zeke asked.

"We'll see," Pa said, throwing a lever and watching the action of the gears. "Hitch 'em up," he told me.

I backed the horses into the shaft, then drove

them ahead slowly while Pa and Zeke walked alongside, watching the gears.

"Ho, lads," Pa called. They stopped instantly. He kicked at one of the large springs but lost his balance and fell against Zeke.

"Let me try," Zeke offered. Pa backed away reluctantly, rubbing his bad leg.

"Take her forward slowly," Zeke said, watching the gears. He gave a sudden sharp kick, metal clanged against metal, and the air was filled with the grinding of heavy machinery.

"Walk on, boys," Pa shouted without a word of gratitude. The horses lurched forward, straining against the added load as the spinning paddles at the rear hurled manure into the air.

"Looks good," Zeke shouted.

"For now," Pa answered, stopping the horses. He climbed up to the seat and told me to drive on. I remained on my feet, watching the sweat build on the horses' thick necks. Pa sat sideways, checking the gears. When we reached the trees, he disengaged the paddles for the turn, then threw them back into gear for the downhill run, the horses gaining speed, the spreader bouncing over the rutted pasture.

The fields had begun to take on color, bright green tufts of onion grass and the first dandelions sprouting amid the brown decay of winter. The air felt thick and warm. Birds sang and darted about, gathering twigs and dead grass; squirrels chattered loudly. The colts bucked and leapt, rearing up on their hind legs in mock combat.

We finished the second pass and returned to the top of the pasture. "Sit," Pa said, stopping the horses. I let the reins go slack and dropped down beside him, looking across the valley. In the distance Halvard and Gregory worked their two spreaders.

"Kitty wants you to go to the city with her."

"What for?" I asked, stunned by the idea. I'd never left Providence, wasn't sure I wanted to.

"Some damn foolishness about wedding clothes." He looked across the valley. "This is one hell of a time to go traveling. If she was planning on marrying that peacock all along, she should have done so weeks ago. City folk may get married in June, but not us. Your mother and I waited until the harvest was in. Gregory had enough sense to do the same. Old Hejdling's losing his grip. Anyway, your cousin wants you to go."

"You don't mind?"

"Course I mind. It's a damned nuisance."

"Will we see Eric?"

"You do as you please."

"When does she want to go?"

"End of the month. You get ten days, understand? If she needs more, that's her affair. You get back here and down to work."

CHAPTER

14

꿍 Two nights later the moon rose yellow and full over the leafless woods. I carried Pa's rifle over my forearm and a box of cartridges in my pocket. Zeke and Pa followed silently behind. The woods smelled damp and rich with decay. Mushrooms sprouted from fallen tree trunks. The dark red cones of skunk cabbage had begun pushing through the sandy stream banks. Patches of icy snow lingered in shadowy hollows.

The day had been warm, but with the sudden cooling of night a thick fog gathered about the trees, turning them gray, coating them with a fine mist. The farther we walked, the more shrouded the moon became until it vanished altogether, taking the silver shadows with it.

"Getting mighty soupy," Zeke whispered. "Can't see ten feet ahead."

"That's what ears are for," Pa said.

The old cabin loomed up suddenly, then dissolved behind us as we crossed the wooded plateau and dropped into the ravine where the raspberries grew. A lone pheasant, startled by our approach, took flight, honking loudly as it disappeared into the fog.

"That would have made a tasty meal," Zeke remarked.

"You always talk this much when hunting?" Pa asked.

"Sometimes talk's just as nourishing as meat," Zeke replied. Pa grunted.

"Shh," I said, squinting through the fog.

Pa and Zeke looked at me in surprise. Something stirred across the lake. I not only heard it, I felt it.

"You make damn sure you know what you're shooting at before you pull that trigger," Pa whispered.

"Wouldn't want to put a bullet through a neighbor by mistake," Zeke added.

A beaver waddled out of the fog, sniffed the raspberry canes, eyed us warily, and slipped into the black water. We waited there a long while, listening to the damp sighing of the woods, the flutter of bats, the occasional hooting of owls, my ears sharply tuned to the night.

"I'm gonna head back," Zeke said finally, backing away quietly. "Good luck."

I didn't regret his going. I wanted to be alone. Something was happening to me. I began to understand Eric's need for solitude.

"You go, too," I said to Pa.

"You sure?" he asked, studying my face.

"Yup."

A faint smile played across his lips. "I'll be just up the top of the ravine."

"No, Pa, go home."

"How you gonna carry a three-hundred-pound buck up and out of here?"

"I don't know." I hadn't thought that far ahead.

"Don't get cocky."

"I'm not. I just can't think with you watching me every second."

"I'll be back by the cabin then," he said, walking off. As his footsteps died away and the woods grew still, I felt a sudden thrill. I was on my own now. I touched the healing scar on my cheek. I was whole. Pa, Eric, Kitty, and Zeke were outside of me. Something solid was taking shape within.

I skirted the swamp and climbed the far side of the ravine, then broke into a run, holding the empty rifle before me, warding off branches as I dodged among the trees. The ground leveled off, the trees grew sparser, the fog began to thin. Then the moon reappeared, dull and insubstantial at first, gradually brightening and growing more solid as I left the trees, crossed an abandoned pasture crowded with waist-high brambles, and entered a newly plowed field, the soft, black earth smelling of onions and manure. My boots sank to the ankles as I jumped from furrow to furrow.

The night was alive with muffled movements. A lone owl leapt from an oak limb and soared noiselessly toward me, casting an eerie gray shadow over the furrows before dropping suddenly to capture a darting field mouse in its talons and winging powerfully back to its perch.

I climbed a huge boulder the size of a small wagon and sat cross-legged at the top, feeling the residue of the sun's warmth on the rock's rough surface. The stars shone feebly through the moist air. I felt like laughing, exhilarated by my new freedom, the darkness no longer foreign and forbidding but rich with possibility.

Long before I saw the buck, I sensed its approach, the skin on my arms and neck bristling with awareness. Slipping a cartridge into the breech, I shouldered the rifle, resting the barrel on my upraised knees. The buck stepped from the underbrush onto the soft, new-plowed earth and paused, his nose testing the air, scenting danger. I watched him through the sight, the tips of my fingers throbbing. Slowly, he walked toward me, pausing to nibble clumps of new grass left unturned by the plow. He came within fifty yards of the boulder and stopped. *You know I'm here, don't you?* I thought, aiming at the center of his thick neck. He sniffed the air, trying to locate the threat, but the wind did not betray me. He took a few tentative steps my way, ears fluttering forward and back, trying to pick up some telltale sound. I leaned into the rifle butt, pressing it hard against my shoulder, held my breath, and slowly squeezed the trigger.

I didn't hear the explosion. The buck rose into the air, turning and leaping in one graceful motion, then plummeted to earth. "Oh my God!" I whispered, slipping off the rock and running toward the buck. He was still panting when I reached him, eyes focused somewhere far beyond me. He tried to rise but succeeded only in moving his head slightly, his heavy antlers plowing more deeply into the earth. Then his legs grew suddenly rigid, the panting stopped, and he was still. In that moment he seemed to shrink, to lose color. I shivered in sudden realization of what I had just done. Where a moment ago life had throbbed, there was now only emptiness, death. I ran my hand over the thick, tawny skin of his powerful neck, still warm and wet with blood, feeling Mama's impulse to hug him and ask forgiveness. "I'm sorry," I whispered.

I set the rifle aside and tried to shoulder the buck, then to drag him, but the huge antlers moored him to the earth as securely as a ship's anchor. Exhausted by the effort, I finally sat down between his outstretched legs, lay my cheek against his soft flank, and breathing in the warm animal aroma and the fragrance of moist earth, dozed off.

———

When I awoke the moon was directly overhead; pale white light pooled around me. Muffled footsteps reverberated through the soft soil. A compact black shape approached, gun slung over one shoulder, hair shining almost white in the moonlight. It was Halvard.

"You out here alone?" he asked as I stood up, still groggy with sleep. I nodded. He circled the buck, whistling his admiration. "Nice shooting. Do you mind?" He took hold of the antlers and gave a tug. "Three hundred pounds easy," he declared. "You need help dressing it?"

"I never did it before," I admitted.

"It's not hard." He unsheathed a large hunting knife and handed it to me, then rolled the buck on his back and showed me where to begin, pointing to a spot just below the rib cage. The hide was tough, but once the knife penetrated the thick skin it cut easily, laying bare the red-and-white organs within. They felt warm in my hands, steaming in the cool air. I dug a hole and buried the remains, scouring my bloodstained fingers with dirt. Then I took hold of the hind legs, Halvard the antlers, and together we dragged the buck toward the rock in the center of the field.

"You think you can shoulder him?" he asked.

"I'll try," I said. He hauled the buck up over the top of the rock, then positioned me with my back to it.

"Brace yourself," he said, laying the hind legs over my left shoulder, the forelegs over my right. "Hold tight and lean forward slowly." As I did, the heavy head left the rock, falling sharply against my back. I staggered under the weight, tried to steady myself with Halvard's help, then collapsed to my knees. He pulled the crushing load from me.

"Maybe I better try," he offered, kneeling beside me. He took the burden upon his own shoulders, standing slowly, feet wide apart. He was not much taller than me but twice as wide. His neck looked as powerful as the buck's.

I took both rifles and walked beside him. At the trees the fog closed in around us. The deeper into the woods we walked, the dimmer the moon grew.

"You okay?" I asked. His face was covered with sweat.

"Winter made me a little soft," he said, panting.

I felt a sudden affection for him. "When are you and Kitty gonna get married?"

"As soon as she'll have me."

We walked on a ways, then he leaned the heavy load against a tree and caught his breath.

"Don't you mind what folks say?"

"About her being too old for me? Not enough to give her up. She's the finest, most capable woman I know. The heart keeps its own counsel, you know. There's reason and then there's feeling. When the two go their separate ways, I generally stick with feeling. How about you?"

"I don't know. I never thought about it."

"You will soon enough." He shrugged the buck more comfortably across his shoulders, then began the steep climb out of the ravine.

At the cabin we found Pa sitting bearlike on the porch steps, his head resting on his knees. When I called his name he shivered, blinked his eyes, then straightened his neck with a crack.

"What you got there?" he asked, squinting at Halvard.

"Your boy's some shot," Halvard declared. Pa rose slowly, pressing both hands against his lower back.

"You dropped him?" he asked me in disbelief.

"I heard the shot," Halvard said.

He studied the neck wound, then the gutting. "Dressed him, too?"

"Halvard showed me how."

"Nate did all the work," Halvard insisted. "He's a natural."

Pa took hold of my chin and rocked it left and right, breaking into a smile. "That's good work, son, real good work. I'm proud of you. Kitty's right. You've got the instinct for this life."

For three weeks we plowed from sunup to sunset, turning over Zeke's newly cleared ground, harrowing the old. I shed my boots, walking bare-foot behind the horses, feeling the cool, damp earth between my toes. It was the first spring Pa let me plow alone. We worked opposite ends of the field, slowly converging upon the center. It took Dart and Doc a week before they cast off their winter lethargy and began pulling with real strength. The first few nights I collapsed into bed before supper, too exhausted to eat, my shoulders and back screaming with pain. But by the end of the second week I was eating as much as Zeke and Pa, then returning to the fields after dark to shoo away the birds pecking at the newly sown seed.

The Hejdlings were working their fields just as feverishly—Gregory, Halvard, Bittle, and even occasionally Mr. Hejdling—driving horse and plow across acres of dormant brown cornfield, turning under the old shoots, planting the new. Whenever I paused to wipe the sweat from my face or to take a long drink from the water pail, my eyes scanned the opposite ridge, measuring our progress against theirs. In my mind we were locked in competition, racing to be the first to get seed into the ground.

At noon each day Kitty brought lunch in a large basket, then sat with us in the greening pasture. Lisa and Sonja did the same across the way, Trudy sometimes joining them, bearing little Ethan in her arms. Once Lisa took the plow from her brothers and cut a row as expertly as they did. Sonja sometimes sat astride one of the horses and rode with them, her ribboned hair all asparkle.

The trees began to burst their buds, dressing themselves in new leaves. The woods grew green and full of shadows, walling in the pasture, filtering the light. One breezy afternoon the white dandelion bolls released their seed in a horizontal blizzard that filled the air with tiny feathers. That same week the ancient apple trees flowered, turning the hillsides white with blossoms.

About that time Kitty weaned Rebel from both the bottle and the house, returning him to the flock. At first he broke away every sunset and lingered outside the kitchen, slipping in whenever the door was left ajar, bleating for handouts when it wasn't. But Kitty was no longer willing to clean up after him. He had long since ceased to be the smallest lamb on the farm. He would never be as large as his brother, but he was growing steadily and producing a thick black coat that was softer and finer than any in the flock. The two brothers didn't spend much time together during the day, but every night they bedded down side by side within reach of their foster mother.

As the weather continued to warm, Bianca exchanged her winter roost for an outside perch above the hayloft door, her feathers blindingly white against the weathered gray siding. "She bears your mother's soul," Kitty declared one afternoon, looking up from her vegetable garden as

Bianca fluttered from sheep pen to hayloft. Kitty had only to give voice to the thought for it to burst full bloom within me. Bianca hovered over us like a loving mother. She might not be able to protect us from harm, but she tried, in her way, to warn us of danger.

Part Three

CHAPTER

15

"Ten days," Pa declared as we neared the river, "not a day more."

"I've left you food enough for twice that," Kitty said. "And there's always Zeke's mutton and maple syrup in a pinch."

"It's not my stomach I'm concerned about. There's haying to do. If we don't get to it by the end of next week, it'll be hell to cut."

"We'll be back," Kitty assured him. Then she pointed through the trees toward the silver water and cried, "There's the river!"

The sun was already high and hot, the air alive with insects. Dart's tail switched lazily against his back. Kitty fanned her face. Despite the June heat, she wore a long navy blue cape, the hood thrown over her head in a futile effort to keep her hair under control.

Near the steamboat pier, the road grew dusty with the traffic of wagons and motorcars. And then suddenly the gleaming white steamship rose up before us, dozens of colored flags snapping from the guy lines, *New Hope* painted in tall black letters over the paddle wheel. A thick plume of steam rose from one of the twin smokestacks. Scores of passengers milled about the three outside decks, waving to friends standing along the riverbank. Dozens of longshoremen loaded cargo. Bells rang, porters shouted.

"We've got a farm to run," Pa said, helping Kitty down while I struggled with her trunk.

"Sometimes you just have to make allowances for life, Uncle Ray."

"Seems all I'm doing these days is making allowances."

"We'll be back as promised."

"You miss that boat, you'll walk back to the farm."

The piercing howl of the ship's whistle filled the air. Everyone about the pier began moving more quickly: passengers scurried up the gangway, visitors hurried down, sailors loosened lines, lashed cargo, shut portholes.

Pa reached into his pocket and pulled out a sealed envelope. "This is for you," he said, handing it to Kitty.

"Uncle Ray!" she cried, her eyes wide with surprise.

"Maggie would have wanted you to get something special for yourself," he said, trying to deflect her thanks. Then to me he added, "You take good care of your cousin. The city's a dangerous place."

I wanted to be done with good-byes. I had barely slept the last two nights, thinking about the moment we would stand on deck watching the ship cast off. It was what Mama had done when she left us.

Seagulls circled overhead, squawking loudly. The air smelled of burning coal and rotting wood. The ship scraped against the dock, rising and falling with the restless river. Everything seemed in flux, bursting with energy, chafing to be set free.

"I'm in good hands," Kitty said, throwing an arm around my shoulder. Then she grabbed Pa's hand and kissed it, thanking him for his gift.

"Get going, before you miss your boat," he said, yanking his hand free.

Kitty locked her arm in mine and strode to the end of the dock. At the foot of the gangway, we joined a long line of passengers waiting to board. Up close the ship wasn't as white as it appeared from a distance. Brown rust ringed the lower portholes, bubbling up beneath the blistered white paint. A green film ringed the boat at water level.

"Tickets, ma'am," the bursar called.

"Tickets, yes, of course," Kitty said with sudden nervousness, handing me the grip. "Tickets, tickets." She peered inside the bag. "I know I packed them."

"Step aside, please," he said impatiently. More

bells sounded. Heavy steel doors slammed shut. The line behind us diminished.

"They must be here somewhere," she muttered, burying her arms up to her elbows in the grip. Then in desperation she threw off her cape and told me to empty the bag on it. I did so, creating a small mountain of combs, hairpins, handkerchiefs, ribbons, food tins, forks, a hand mirror, a change of clothes, and finally, at the bottom, a small purse. Kitty tore it open and, with a sigh of relief, produced the two bent tickets. A moment later we stepped from the pier to the slanting gangway and climbed toward a black hole in the side of the ship, the wooden planks bouncing beneath our feet.

The dark hold we entered was crammed with wooden crates, their destinations painted in large letters on the side. A sailor dressed in white welcomed us aboard and directed us to an iron stairway. We climbed into the light of the lower promenade deck, where hundreds of passengers crowded the rail, waving to people below.

I squeezed through the throng and looked for Pa, but he had already turned the wagon around and headed home.

"Most impatient man I've ever known," Kitty said, squeezing in beside me. "Not even a 'bon voyage.' Well, never mind." She threw her hood back and waved to the crowd of strangers below, shouting, "Good-bye, good-bye."

A few late-arriving passengers hurried aboard.

The wheelhouse bell sounded three times. Below us the crew began to pull the gangway onto the dock. More steel doors slammed. Sailors fore and aft released thick, braided ropes from the pier. Then, with nothing binding us to land, the ship's whistle blew loud and long.

"Don't lean over so far," Kitty said, taking hold of my arm as I looked down at the widening black gulf between ship and shore.

"We're moving!" I cried. Somewhere deep below our feet the heart of the ship began to beat. A great belch of smoke rose from the twin smokestacks as the huge paddle wheel turned, digging deep into the black river and rising again, trailing streams of foaming white water.

"Isn't it wonderful?" Kitty shouted over the noise. The ship gradually gained speed, the land slipped away, the dock grew smaller. Then we rounded a bend in the river and everything familiar was gone. Before us lay a new world.

"Let's go up front," I said, pulling Kitty through the crowd. The ship's prow cut neatly through the river, splintering the water into a thousand tiny droplets that glistened in the sunlight.

"Isn't this glorious," she declared, holding to the railing with both hands. "It feels like we're flying. I'm sorry Uncle Ray isn't here. A change like this would do him a world of good."

I couldn't imagine Pa anywhere but Providence.

As the ship carved a path through the river, seagulls glided overhead, their motionless, outstretched wings nearly transparent against the sun. "I want to explore the other decks," I shouted into the wind.

"Go ahead. Just be careful." Kitty gave me the number of our cabin and told me to meet her there in an hour, then faced back into the wind, her wind-ravaged hair snapping behind her.

I stepped from the promenade deck over a high doorsill into a crowded observation room lined with wicker chairs and potted palms, the roar of the wind replaced by the clamor of conversation, clanking dishes, and strolling musicians. At the rear I climbed another set of stairs to the cabin deck, then continued up to the very top of the ship. There beside the towering smokestacks a huge steel piston rose and fell, driving the paddle wheel. Near the bow the captain stood in a glass-enclosed wheelhouse, scanning the river traffic as he guided the ship downstream, his hands resting on a great wooden wheel.

At the stern I watched our long, white wake roll outward to both shores, rocking the small boats moored along the banks. Then I descended to the lowest deck, where the shiny copper and brass fixtures gave way to rusting iron and the acrid smell of brine. I felt uneasy down there. No windows let in the light. Behind closed doors marked "engine room" and "boiler room," the

machinery that powered the ship roared fero-
ciously. The river slapped against the white walls,
feeling dangerously close. I kept the steps in sight,
trying to fend off a rising panic, then bolted upstairs as though assailed by some terrible demon,
my heart pounding.

When I finally reached our cabin, I found Kitty
sitting on the lower of two bunk beds, brushing
her hair. One wall of the windowless room was
taken up by our beds, another by a mahogany
closet, a third by a small sink and a door to a tiny
toilet and shower. All the wooden surfaces were
carefully polished; all the brass and steel fittings
gleamed.

"It's not exactly spacious," Kitty observed, "but
it's comfy."

I climbed to the upper berth and touched the
metal ceiling above my head, feeling the ship's
vibrations in my fingertips. I wondered if Mama
had died in a room like this.

"What would we do if the ship started to
sink?" I asked Kitty.

"That's a terrible thought!"

"Could we get out in time?"

"Of course we could."

"Mama didn't."

"But everyone else did."

"Why couldn't she?" I asked, pounding the
steel ceiling.

"I wish I knew."

That night Kitty and I shared a table with an elderly, bearded man in a dark suit and a younger man wearing white linen trousers, a matching jacket, and a straw hat. The older man introduced himself as Mr. Stiles and identified the other as his son Benjamin. The father smiled warmly as he spoke; the son barely acknowledged us, his eyes following the violinist who strolled among the tables playing Viennese waltzes.

"Doesn't he play beautifully," Kitty remarked, her face aglow.

"Is this your first river voyage?" Mr. Stiles asked.

"For both of us," Kitty admitted.

"Wonderful, isn't it? So much more gracious than traveling by rail."

"Do you sail often?" Kitty asked.

"I've lost track of how many steamer voyages I've taken," he said, stroking his glossy gray beard. "What would you say, Ben—fifty, sixty?"

His son had pushed his chair back from the table and was languidly smoking a cigarette as he surveyed the bustling, sun-filled room. "You would know better than I, Father," he replied with an indifferent air, inhaling deeply, then releasing the smoke from the corners of his mouth as though it required too great an effort to blow it out.

"Benjamin does not share my enthusiasm for steamships," Mr. Stiles observed. "But he is kind enough to indulge his aging father from time to time. He much prefers the speed of the rails, don't you, son?" Benjamin didn't bother to respond. "He can't understand why, if one can make the same trip by rail in one quarter of the time, anyone would bother traveling by boat. The romance escapes him. But not you, Miss Burns, I trust?"

"I think it's thrilling," she said, studying the elegantly dressed passengers, the potted palms, the stewards in their gleaming white coats, the sparkling water glasses, the shining silverware.

"It *is* thrilling, my dear, most thrilling experience I know, a tonic for flagging spirits. Whenever I begin to feel dull, I head for the nearest steamship. It never fails to restore me. Shall we order?"

After supper most of the passengers moved into one of the glass-enclosed lounges. I circled the nearly empty deck at sunset, taking the wind full in my face. A woman stood alone at the prow, watching the river turn orange. Something about her struck me as warmly familiar. I felt a sudden urge to see her face. As I came up beside her, my heart began to beat in my throat. Her neck, the shape of her ears, the knotted hair at the back of her head—a cry leapt to my throat. I reached forward to touch her arm. A voice called, "Stephanie!" and the woman turned around. It wasn't Mama. She didn't look anything like her. She smiled at me, then walked away. I took her place at the rail and stared vacantly into the darkening river, trembling.

Far to the south a steamer approached, its upper deck twinkling with electric lights. Along the banks, windows cast their yellow lamplight onto the water. A band began to play on the deck below.

I followed the music to a vast salon at the rear of the ship crowded with passengers smoking and dancing. Mr. Stiles sat in a corner with a man roughly his own age but much heavier, both enjoying thick cigars and drinking from large goblets. Mr. Stiles did most of the talking, his amiable listener grunting from time to time in agreement, occasionally flicking the ash from his cigar into a shell-shaped ashtray or taking another sip from his glass. I stood near enough to hear, dazzled by all the commotion.

"Most romantic sight I know," Mr. Stiles mused, watching the approaching steamer pass us all ablaze, its lights reflected in the river.

"She is a lovely thing, isn't she," the other replied. "Reminds me of the *Holly Fair*. What a glory she was."

"You knew her?" Mr. Stiles asked.

"Nearly went down with her," the wider man replied, inhaling deeply on his cigar.

"Terrible loss. Beautiful ship."

My eyes fastened on them; all other conversation in the room seemed to cease. The *Holly Fair* was the steamer that sank with Mama aboard.

"Can't recall a more promising voyage," the stouter man said, "calm seas, tide running with us. We keep a summer place upriver, a little farm. Mrs. Wells doesn't care for it much, but the children do. Well, they did. They're quite a bit older now. The boys are on their own and my daughter just married."

Mr. Stiles congratulated the man and encouraged him to resume his story.

"We were standing at the prow, Mrs. Wells and I—I always like to stand up front when we leave port, feel the wind in my face, smell the salt air. My wife doesn't care for it. Complains it stickies up her hair."

Mr. Stiles nodded and smiled.

"The river was bustling that day. Never saw so many barges and yachts. Ship was so crowded there wasn't a spare inch along the rail. When my wife gave up her spot to go comb her hair, quite a tussle developed between two young sports intent on taking her place. They practically came to blows."

"And the accident?" Mr. Stiles prodded.

"Easily avoided. I remember saying to a chap next to me, 'Captain ought to take care off the port bow. That barge is not yielding.' A moment later the whistle sounded and the engines reversed, rattling the ship terribly. But it was too late. I was thrown forward against the rail as we collided. There was a great squealing and scraping, and then everything was deathly still."

"Were you hurt?" Mr. Stiles asked.

"Winded only, though some of the other passengers were a bit bruised. Then all sorts of whistles and bells began to sound. The whole ship started listing sharply to port. There was quite a bit of pushing and shoving. The captain made a gallant effort to get us back into harbor, but the ship wouldn't respond. The barge had torn through three watertight compartments, flooding them."

"Was there any panic?" Mr. Stiles prodded.

"Nothing of consequence. It was quite orderly, actually. They lowered the lifeboats with great haste and signaled to shore for assistance. Within minutes we were taken off the ship. Barely got our feet wet. Mrs. Wells claimed a new pair of pumps were ruined and she seemed to have misplaced her boa in all the commotion, but otherwise we escaped without a scratch, riding back to shore with a merry little band of fellow survivors, who thought it quite the best entertainment they'd had in a long while. Most of them boarded the two o'clock steamer and continued on their way, but I could not persuade Mrs. Wells to do the same. She hasn't been afloat since."

"Was there no loss of life?" Mr. Stiles asked. "I thought I read . . . "

My eyes focused on Mr. Wells's mouth, catching each word as it fell from his lips.

"Three dead, I believe, or was it four? I don't recall now. Fortunately only one passenger, a woman traveling alone; the rest were ship's hands, trapped below deck. One doesn't feel quite so bad in their case, does one? I mean, it's a risk they take, an occupational hazard, so to speak. But that poor woman . . . "

I felt my skin bristle.

"Didn't she try to save someone?" Mr. Stiles asked.

"I believe so. Something having to do with a missing child. I didn't witness any of it myself, mind you, there was so much commotion. Apparently the poor woman gave up her place in the lifeboat to look for the lost child, then got trapped below deck when the bulkhead gave way."

Tears sprang to my eyes.

"And the missing child?"

"Some other passenger had taken him in hand and carried him to shore. He was never in any real danger."

I ran from the crowded room, taking refuge against the rail. If only she hadn't left the lifeboat. It wasn't fair. She should have been rewarded for her bravery, not punished. Why did she have to die?

I stood out in the wind a long time, studying the stars and trying to understand. When I finally turned in, Kitty was already lying in her berth reading.

"I was beginning to think you fell overboard," she chided. "What's wrong with your eyes?"

"Nothing," I said, wiping them.

"Nathan, come here," she said, studying my face. I shook my head, trying to cast off the suffocating pressure building in my chest.

"Nate, what is it?"

A great sob rose to my throat, heaving my shoulders. Kitty threw her arms around me.

"Is it your mother?" she asked, stroking my head.

She had only to say it for the knot in my chest to come untied and the pressure to ease. Between sobs I told her what I had just heard. We talked until after midnight.

"She died a hero," Kitty said.

"But the boy was safe," I moaned, feeling the pointlessness of her death all over again.

"But she didn't know that," Kitty insisted. "She did a brave and wonderful thing."

I shook my head, unable to shed the bitterness of it, muttering, "Why did she have to die?"

The ship's massive heart throbbed mournfully in my ears.

CHAPTER

16

❧ I slept little that night, thinking of Mama's pointless death, wondering why it had to happen. Every time I drifted off, I was awakened by the reverberations of the ship's engine, the slamming of cabin doors, and the noise of passengers in the hall. Kitty, too, slept lightly and was up so early the next morning that we decided to go out on deck and watch the sun rise.

We passed through one of the large observation rooms crowded with people asleep on benches and chairs, their arms dangling at their sides or stuffed deep within pockets, their mouths open, breathing deeply. The shore beyond the windows was thickly settled with small farms and towns. A freight train labored south, trailing a long, thin line of smoke. The clatter of boxcars drifted over the water. Distant church bells rang the hour. Dozens of small fishing boats were already afloat, casting their nets upon the water. Seagulls glided a few inches above the glassy surface, then soared aloft, catching the sunlight on the underside of their wings.

"How do you feel?" Kitty asked.

"Hollow."

Kitty threw an arm around my shoulder and murmured, "I know," then pointed downriver to a glittering forest of glass and steel and said with sudden animation, "There it is!"

"New York?" I asked. It seemed a trick of light—insubstantial, dreamlike.

"That's it. We better eat before the mob awakes."

We took our seats in the nearly empty dining room, the aroma of pancakes and bacon whetting my appetite. When the steward offered Kitty coffee, I asked for some as well. Kitty looked at me in astonishment. "Now don't you grow up on me all of a sudden just because we're nearing the city."

"You don't have to worry about me anymore," I said into my coffee cup. "I can take care of myself."

"Where have I heard that before?"

"I don't mean it the way Eric does. I just mean, I'm okay now."

"I understand."

"Not just about Mama. I mean you don't have to worry about getting married."

Kitty laid her hand on mine and smiled.

After breakfast Kitty returned to the cabin to pack her grip and freshen up while I stood at the prow, watching the city approach. Motorcars raced south along the shore road, steamships and barges churned the water white, sailboats filled the air with snapping canvas. The colossal buildings grew taller. Every inch of riverbank seemed occupied by piers and warehouses. Huge winches loaded and unloaded cargo ships. Whistles and bells sounded as crowded ferries crossed from one shore to the other, passengers standing shoulder to shoulder on windy decks, some staring at the dark water, others trying to read carefully folded newspapers buffeted by the wind.

Just as Kitty joined me, clutching her grip, the steamer began to slow. Our whistle sounded and we began turning sideways to the current. For a moment the rhythmic pulse of the engine stopped, then reversed as we began backing into port, the black water churning forward, sending bits of decayed wood and seaweed floating out beyond the prow. The first hawser sailed from the stern and was pulled ashore by two longshoremen, who ran with it to the farthest tackle. Half-a-dozen more lines arced through the air, each helping to secure the heavy ship to the wooden pier. Doors clanged open, the gangway was shoved into the side of the hull, and suddenly passengers began to disembark, hailing friends and hackney drivers. Beyond the docks rose windowless warehouses and towering skyscrapers.

"Just look at it!" Kitty exclaimed, holding me back. "Isn't it wonderful!" The morning light ricocheted off a thousand shiny surfaces.

"Let's go," I said, eager to get ashore.

"It's not going to run away, Nate. We've got ten days to enjoy it."

"Nine," I corrected.

Still she lingered.

"I'll see you ashore," I finally said, running down the stairs muttering, "Excuse me," as I pushed my way onto the gangway and down to the pier. Passengers, longshoremen, and cabbies crowded around the luggage as it was unloaded from the ship's hold.

"Kitty," I cried, waving to her.

She waved back, still studying the skyline.

"Come down!"

"I'm coming," she said, leaving the rail. We gathered our bags and hired a motor taxi to drive us to our hotel, Kitty giggling with pleasure as the cab roared off, bumping over the cobblestones.

"First visit to the city?" the driver asked, looking back over his shoulder. He wore a threadbare tweed jacket and a tan cap over bushy, sand-colored hair.

"It's been a long time," Kitty said, gazing out the window at the crowd of people hurrying to work. We passed into a kind of tunnel open on both sides but partially covered overhead by wooden slats that painted the road before us in white stripes of sunlight.

"Staying long?" the driver asked.

"About a week," Kitty responded.

"That's time enough to see the city. I'm at your service whenever you need a car." He reached into his jacket and pulled out a small card with his name and phone number printed on it. "That's my home. Call anytime. The wife'll answer if I'm not there. I can show you all the sights."

"You've got your own telephone?" I asked.

"Wife's idea. It's an expense, but you got to have one these days; everybody does."

As he spoke an ominous rumbling began to build somewhere behind us, growing steadily louder, until I thought we were about to be run down by some huge and terrible engine. My eyes darted between the driver and Kitty, but they talked on, hardly noticing the roar. And then it exploded above us. I ducked as a dark shadow raced over the top of the car, trembling the earth.

The driver laughed. "It's only the el."

"The elevated subway," Kitty explained.

I sat back in my seat, feeling both foolish and amazed. There were more wonders in this city than one could count.

We left the unnatural darkness of the elevated train trestles, returning to the light with a sudden burst of speed that carried us along a street lined with identical brown buildings rising five and six stories. The wind whistled through the car. Children played on front stoops, mothers sat in open windows, taxis and private motorcars hurried by, horns honking.

"It's better than an amusement park," Kitty declared, turning her head from side to side. We rounded another corner and pulled up before a red-brick hotel called the Harbor House. I craned my head back, counting twelve floors.

"How do people get up there?" I asked, pointing to the top.

"Wings," the driver said, removing our trunk and dragging it toward the door. "Did you bring yours?"

A young man dressed in tight-fitting blue pants and a matching vest took the trunk and carried it inside. Kitty paid the driver, then followed the bellhop into the hotel. We registered at the front desk before entering a small iron cage that shut with a clang and rose slowly through a dark shaft, chains rattling above and below us. My stomach quivered when the cage started and again when it stopped.

At the eighth floor the bellhop threw open the gate and led us down a dimly lit hallway carpeted in red and hung with gilt-framed photographs of three-masted schooners. Small electric lights burned behind seashell shades. From the dark hall we stepped into a sunlit room decorated with plush sofas and thick-armed chairs. I ran to the window and looked down from the dizzying height upon a world of toy cars and carriages.

"Don't lean out so far," Kitty said, handing the bellhop a coin.

"It's a long way down," the young man said stepping back into the hall. "Enjoy your stay."

"We're practically in the clouds," I said.

"Almost," Kitty replied. "After I freshen up, we'll try to find that bohemian brother of yours."

I stood at the window watching the tumult below: carriages and motorcars streamed by, the rattle of engines and the clop of horseshoes echoing off the buildings across the street. The city was a living thing, people, horses, and machines in constant motion, buildings belching black clouds of soot as though breathing, elevated trains thumping in the distance like great metal arteries, the whir of the hotel's elevators seeping through the walls. On the broad avenue, streetcars clanged, their steel wheels screeching at every turn. Double-decker buses rolled by, the upper decks open to the sky, passengers clinging to hats and flapping scarves. Pedestrians hurried along the white sidewalks, crossing the street at a thousand different places, barely escaping catastrophe. Just watching it all was exhausting.

We left the hotel and quickly found ourselves among a throng of smart-looking people hurrying in every direction. Kitty nodded at passersby and stopped occasionally to peer into shop windows and restaurants. After several blocks we caught sight of the imposing stone facade of the Art Academy, the four corners dominated by crenelated towers that pierced the blue sky.

"Does Eric know we're coming?" I asked.

"I wrote him."

"Did he write back?"

"Of course not."

We passed beneath a high stone arch inscribed with the words "Art for the Sake of Life, Life for the Sake of Art" and found ourselves in a large green courtyard crisscrossed by gravel paths. Young men wearing scarves instead of ties and soft caps instead of hats crossed before us in a continuous stream, smoking pipes and cigars, carrying large white pads and boxes of charcoal, their fingers stained black. Several eyed us with curiosity, exchanging smiles; others seemed lost in thought. Kitty stopped one and asked if he knew Eric Burns and where we might find him. Without replying the student pointed toward a ground-floor window and hurried on with an air of self-importance.

"Isn't it exciting?" Kitty whispered. "So much talent concentrated in one place."

We entered a dark, noisy hallway crowded with still more young men talking in groups. Kitty asked again for Eric and was directed to an open door blocked by several more students peering over each other's shoulders in an effort to see what was going on inside.

"Excuse me," Kitty said, tapping one of them on the back. "I'm looking for Eric Burns."

"He's got the best seat in the house," the young man replied, pointing with his chin toward the center of the room.

"For what?" Kitty asked.

"Life drawing," the student replied, his eyes still fixed on something inside. "They should be breaking soon. They're already five minutes over."

As he spoke, students began to file out into the hall. When the room had emptied, we stepped inside. The stale, hot air was blue with tobacco smoke. A few students remained, their low stools arranged in a semicircle around an elevated wooden platform. Eric's profile faced us, a large pad of white paper resting upon a small easel before him. His right hand moved rapidly across it. He wore the same white shirt and dark vest of the other students and chewed absently on the stem of a cold pipe. The faint shadow of a mustache darkened his upper lip.

Kitty signaled me to be quiet as she tiptoed to his shoulder. I followed, but she turned suddenly and tried to bar my way. But I had already glimpsed Eric's drawing: a young woman standing naked, arms raised, drying her hair with a towel. As I tried to see it more clearly, I accidentally bumped Eric's arm.

"Damn," he shouted, turning around in anger.

A streak of black charcoal cut the finely drawn figure in half.

"I'm sorry," I said, backing away. He glared at me, then at Kitty, showing no surprise, just rage.

"I'm sorry," I repeated, feeling a mixture of humiliation and annoyance. This was not the way I had envisioned our reunion.

"It's ruined," Eric said, slamming his pipe down on the easel and standing. He had grown several inches since leaving home.

"No, it's not," Kitty said. "You can fix it."

"Sure I can," he sneered. He tore the drawing from his pad, ripped it in half, and tossed the pieces to the floor. Then, without giving it or us another thought, he gathered up his charcoals and pulled his jacket from a peg on the wall. As he did, a young woman emerged from behind a screen. She did not wear a long, full skirt and blouse like Kitty but a short white dress that barely covered her knees. And instead of a hat she wore around her forehead a silver band that sparkled in the window light. I recognized her boyish short hair as that of Eric's model. Kitty's eyes followed her out of the room, where three young men waited to accompany her down the hall.

"Pretty girl," Kitty remarked. Eric snorted as he filled his pipe from a bag in his jacket pocket. It made him look both older and vaguely foolish. "Doesn't she catch cold standing like that?" Kitty probed, reddening.

"She's used to it."

"Isn't she embarrassed?" I asked.

"Why should she be?"

"I would be."

"That's because you're an ignorant farm boy."

"Would *you* stand up there naked?" I challenged.

"Yes," he replied defiantly.

"Oh sure!"

"Why not?"

"Because it's . . . indecent," Kitty declared. "Why would anyone do a thing like that?"

"To eat," he said scowling, then walked out of the room with his pad under one arm. The hallway was nearly empty, but the courtyard had filled with students lying on the grass, eating lunch, and smoking. Several hailed Eric as he passed.

"You wouldn't really do that, would you?" Kitty asked again when we reached the street.

"It's one way to pay the rent," he said.

"I'm afraid to ask about the others."

"I wash dishes and sweep out the studio of one of the finest artists in the country."

"Where are we going?" Kitty asked breathlessly, trying to keep up with his hurried pace.

"To get some lunch."

"We'd like to take you out, if you have the time," she panted.

"I don't."

"Aren't you in the least bit happy to see us?" she asked.

"I didn't ask you to come."

"Your graciousness overwhelms me."

We walked on in silence, the buildings growing shabbier, the streets dirtier. Wash hung from lines strung across narrow alleys, ash cans stood open on the curb. In the middle of the block Eric turned and mounted a steep flight of steps. From the sidewalk Kitty called after him, "You could show a little common decency and invite us in."

"It's six flights up," he said without turning around.

"I don't care if it's sixty."

"You will."

"Come on," she said to me, following him into a dark and smelly hallway. We mounted to the second floor, then to the third, Kitty breathing hard, calling out as she climbed, "You do this every day?"

"Several times."

She pressed on, leaning against the banister, rapidly slowing, then stopping to catch her breath. "Go," she panted. I hurried to catch up with Eric, who took the stairs two at a time. The bare bulb on the top landing had gone out, but a dusty skylight shed a thin, gray light over the dirty floor. Eric dug deep into his pocket and removed a key. I realized in that moment just how independent he was. He had his own home, could come and go as he pleased with no one to tell him when to get up, when to go to sleep, what to eat.

He pushed open the door and walked in ahead of me, flipping on an electric light. I had expected a room like the one we shared at home, hardly big enough for two beds. Instead we entered a richly decorated living room, the walls hung with paintings, the floor covered with ornate rugs. The center of the room was dominated by a deep couch covered in red velvet. Near the windows stood a large easel with an unfinished canvas in dazzling colors. It took me a moment to recognize the colorful shapes as the buildings across the street and laundry flapping in the wind. The whole city lay beyond Eric's window, offering him a clear view of the endless plain of stone, glass, and brick that stretched to the horizon.

"What a wonderful room," Kitty wheezed, holding the door frame with one hand and her chest with other. "Is all this yours?"

"None of it," Eric replied.

"None of it?"

"Except a few of the paintings. I'm renting it from another student."

"Where is he?"

"In Paris, studying with real artists."

"What do you mean by 'real'?"

"Men who understand painting, not the idiots we have for teachers."

"And when he returns?"

"I'll find another place. It's a big city."

Kitty surveyed the room, moving slowly from painting to painting. They ranged in size and subject from a tiny watercolor no bigger than a postage stamp of two oranges, to a life-size portrait of a young boy dressed in a matador's costume. There were studies of wildflowers and mountains, the profile of a blind man, a streetcar teeming with passengers, a dead pheasant hanging upside down from a door, a table strewn with playing cards, a newborn baby lying naked among pillows, a derelict begging coins on a street corner.

"Did you paint all these?" Kitty asked.

"Most of them," Eric replied, opening the door to his tiny bedroom. There, as at home, his sketches were scattered about the room. Dirty clothes lay heaped in a corner beside the bed. A dusty window looked out upon a gloomy, echoing air shaft. He tossed his pad and charcoals on the unmade bed, then pulled the door shut. I wondered how it would feel to live there alone. It seemed thrilling by day, but I could imagine a frightening loneliness seeping in after dark.

"Did you do this, too?" Kitty asked, pointing to a small bronze statue of a man sitting naked on a rock, one muscular arm clasping an ankle, the other covering his mouth. It struck me as terribly sad.

"No, Westfield."

"Who's that?" Kitty asked.

"Alexander Westfield," he repeated with disdain.

"Oh," she said, shrugging and looking wide-eyed at me.

"I sweep out his studio."

"Oh, him. Do you like his work?" From her tone I guessed that she didn't.

"He was only fourteen when he cast it."

"Precocious."

"Genius," Eric shot back. "I'm hungry and I've only got half an hour."

"Lead the way," Kitty insisted.

We ate in a small restaurant a few blocks from Eric's apartment—the one he washed dishes at twice a week—sitting at a table in a window just below street level, watching all kinds of shoes walk past. After ordering, Eric lapsed into silence. Kitty studied him awhile, then observed, "You haven't asked how your father is."

"How is he?" Eric asked flatly.

"Fine," she replied. "Well, not so fine, really. His leg bothers him terribly lately. He hasn't been himself since you left."

Eric grunted.

"I'm sure he'd appreciate hearing from you from time to time."

"I'm too busy."

"Eric, he's your father!"

"He made my life a misery, drove our mother away, killed her."

"He didn't kill her," Kitty said.

"She drowned," I said.

"I know how she died," Eric replied. "I can read. She wanted to die."

"No, she didn't," I insisted. "She was trying to save someone."

He grew scornful. "No one needed to be saved. They told her to go back to the lifeboats. It was the crew's job to look for missing passengers, not hers. But she just pushed her way past like a madwoman."

"She did not," I insisted.

"It's in all the reports. Go read them yourself. They thought she was crazy."

"She wanted to save that child," I insisted.

"Then why did she hide on the lowest deck, where the sailors couldn't find her?"

"She didn't hide."

"Yes, she did. They found her in a closet. What was she doing there, with the door closed? She didn't want anyone to find her. She *wanted* to drown."

"She did not," I growled, filled with the urge to grab him by the neck.

"She killed herself because she couldn't stand to live with Pa anymore," he sneered.

I burst from my seat and lunged for his face, but his longer arms blocked me.

"Nathan, stop that," Kitty cried, looking around the nearly empty restaurant. "What's the matter with you?"

Tears of rage ran down my cheeks as Eric forced me back into my chair.

"You believe whatever you want," he said, letting go of me. "I don't care."

"She was coming back home to us, that's what I believe," I said. "She was trying to save that little boy. That's the way Mama was."

He snorted contemptuously and turned to the window.

"Why are you so cruel?" Kitty asked him. "Why do you want to poison Nate's mind against your father and sully your mother's memory? You don't know what happened to her with any more certainty than he does."

"You didn't even know her," he snapped.

"I know a woman's heart, and I can certainly understand the terror of losing a child. Your mother did a heroic thing. She tried to help a desperate mother."

My heart swelled as Kitty spoke, but Eric wasn't listening. He ate his lunch in silence, then rose suddenly and said he had to get back to the academy, hurrying away from the table without looking at either of us.

CHAPTER

17

We returned to the hotel after lunch, unpacked our trunk, then took a long walk up the avenue past countless shops and restaurants, all but forgetting about Eric in the rush of new sights and sounds. Vendors hawked fresh fruits and nuts on street corners, beggars sang for coins, acrobats tumbled in vacant alleys before knots of curious onlookers. At five o'clock great hordes of people spilled from the stone and steel buildings lining the streets, walking so fast they seemed to outrun the crowded streetcars. Everyone was in a great hurry to get somewhere, their eyes focused on some distant shore.

"Isn't it exciting?" Kitty remarked, thrilled by all the commotion.

After a lavish dinner of raw oysters, clam chowder, and lobster, Kitty spent an hour soaking in our huge tub. "This is heavenly!" she called from behind the closed bathroom door. "I've never felt so clean."

As night fell I watched the city transform itself into a glittering electric jewel, lights twinkling in thousands of windows and in bright glass globes along every avenue and street. Gradually the traffic grew thinner, the streets quieter. But the city never fell silent. All night dots of red and white light rattled over the cobblestones. Shortly after midnight a man in a tattered coat and hat walked jaggedly across the street, singing loudly. Overhead a single bright star shone in the narrow corridor of sky visible between the tall buildings. I wondered if Pa could see that same star. It didn't seem possible that this noisy, restless city shared the same sky as our quiet farm.

For the next week Kitty and I toured the city, visiting shops and museums, attending Broadway plays and vaudeville shows, symphony concerts, and an opera by Richard Wagner that seemed to last the whole night. One morning Kitty dragged me into a department store about four times larger than the Hejdlings' barn. Dresses, suits, and hats hung from racks covering the vast marble floor. Garlands of flowers wound around thick columns supporting the ceiling. Elegantly dressed women moved rapidly about the floor, skirts rustling, pressing fabrics between their fingers, holding dresses up before mirrors.

"I may not be able to get your father into a decent suit for my wedding," Kitty explained over the persistent ringing of bells and the deafening chatter of customers, "but I expect you to do me proud." For the next two hours I was made to stand before a three-sided mirror, holding my arms up or out or at my sides while a little man with a foreign accent and a cup full of pins measured my arms and legs, neck, waist, and chest and muttered "precisely" while Kitty explained exactly what she wanted.

After the fitting, we ate lunch by the river, watching seagulls dive and soar. "Cheeky devils," Kitty said, and smiled as one alighted a few inches from her, squawking for a handout. "Everything in this city is so bold."

The river and the passing steamers reminded me of Mama. "I want to read those newspaper stories Eric talked about," I declared, squinting into the sun.

"They won't tell you anything you don't already know," Kitty said softly, studying my face.

"I still want to see them for myself."

"They'll only cause you pain. Your mother was coming home to you, Nate. If she had wanted to drown, she could have just thrown herself in the river. She didn't need a sinking steamer or the city, for that matter, to do it." She squeezed my knee.

"Eric doesn't think so."

"Eric needs to believe he's all alone in the world, abandoned and unloved."

"I still want to read them."

"That famous Burns stubbornness beginning to

rear its ugly head, is it?" she said with a pinched expression. "Well, if you're so set on it, you might just try the public library. They usually keep copies of old newspapers. But we can't waste a whole day on it. There's still so much to do."

"I'll go tomorrow morning."

"If you must," she said, brushing the crumbs from her skirt. "Come, we'll be late for the art show." Thanks to a small advertisement in the newspaper, Kitty had discovered that the academy's annual student art exhibition opened that afternoon.

We hailed a cab and returned to Eric's school, finding all the nearby streets crowded with carriages and motorcars discharging passengers in fancy furs and top hats, all headed to the show. We waited almost an hour before being admitted into the vast exhibition hall.

A long table piled high with wine, fruit, and cheese stood in the center of the room. The visitors passed quickly around the perimeter, admiring the paintings, then headed for the food. We looked for Eric as the throng pushed us along past studies of flowers, portraits of children, landscapes with shepherds, and cathedrals. A young man dressed in white walked just ahead of us, ticking off the names of celebrated artists being imitated as he passed each painting, complaining in a too-loud voice that there wasn't a spark of originality anywhere in the room.

At the far end of the hall, we encountered a

logjam almost as dense as the one around the refreshment table. "Excuse me," the pompous young man said, trying to push his way forward, but the crowd refused to give way. Here, as outside Eric's life-drawing class, young men stood on tiptoe, craning their necks to get a better view.

"What's everyone looking at?" Kitty asked.

"The Burns nude, of course," the young man in white said disdainfully.

Nearby, a dusty-looking man holding a pen and a small tablet was questioning a member of the faculty.

"No, as a matter of fact," the teacher remarked, "he's one of our youngest students. Quite precocious."

"What kind of training did he have before coming to the academy?" the reporter asked.

The teacher laughed. "He's a farm boy, wholly self-taught. I doubt if his parents know the difference between a goat and a Gainsborough. Remarkable natural talent, though still quite raw. You'll notice the awkwardness about the hands and feet, some difficulty with perspective, but overall a very promising beginning."

I pushed my way into the crowd, squeezing between two overweight women holding fans over their mouths. When I raised my eyes to the wall, I found myself staring at Lisa Hejdling, completely naked except for a daisy ring around one finger. Her body glistened from her morning swim, glowing a soft, translucent brown in the warm light. You could feel the wetness and the slight chill that prickled her skin. Her cold blue eyes glared back defiantly, challenging the crowd to condemn her brazenness. If her hands and feet were slightly out of proportion, hardly anyone noticed or cared, for the rest of the life-size portrait was so arresting. She was cold and defiant and breathtakingly beautiful.

Kitty stood for a long moment with her gloved hands to her face, then finally muttered, "How could he?"

"What's wrong?" I asked.

"How could he do such a thing? What if Lisa were to see it? It's such a violation."

"Everyone says it's beautiful."

"They're all smirking," she whispered, looking around. "How would you feel if you found yourself up there on the wall, stark naked, leered at by all the world? I'd never be able to show my face again. How am I going to explain this to Halvard and his father? It's hard enough overcoming the obstacles your father has set in our path without Eric adding to them."

"Why do they have to know?"

"You can't keep something like this a secret. By tomorrow it'll be mentioned in all the papers."

"But no one knows who she is."

"Oh no? Look there." Kitty pointed to the white card posted beside the painting. Eric had titled the painting *"Lisa."*

"About the only thing he left off was her

address," she remarked, breaking into a smile. "He's so wicked . . . but very talented."

Kitty pulled me from the painting and out into the courtyard, where other visitors had gone to escape the smoke and noise of the gallery. She asked several passing students if they had seen Eric. One suggested we check the painting studio and pointed us toward it. We found the large room at the end of a dark, empty hallway, the door ajar. Dozens of easels stood clustered around a small platform. Others faced the walls. Eric stood in a distant corner, his back to the door, several brushes protruding from his left hand, one between his teeth. His right hand worked rapidly, confidently, adding color to the canvas.

I approached cautiously, Kitty following, trying to get a glimpse of the large painting over his shoulder. It was another portrait, this time of three figures—himself, Pa, and me—sitting on the steps of the old cabin, staring off into the distance, the setting sun shimmering in our troubled eyes. Pa sat with one leg drawn up, the other, his bad one, outstretched upon the stairs. I sat beside him, one hand gripping his forearm. Eric stood behind us, detached, angry. I could feel Mama hovering just beyond the edge of the canvas, the cause of our anger and grief.

Sensing my approach, Eric turned swiftly and asked with unmasked annoyance, "How did you get in here?"

"The door was open," Kitty explained. "Eric,

it's magnificent." She seemed on the verge of tears.

"It's not finished."

"But it's wonderful."

"It's awful."

"Why do you say that?"

"Because it is."

"He's right, you know," a strange voice interrupted. A bearded, heavyset man pushed his way into the room, nearly knocking several easels over. He walked directly to Eric's canvas. "You still haven't got the leg right. Look there." He pointed to the figure of Pa. "That toe's the size of a grapefruit."

"I know," Eric said with annoyance.

"Excuse me," Kitty said, offering her hand, "I'm Eric's cousin Kitty and this is his brother, Nathan."

"Alexander Westfield," the huge man said, still facing Eric. "Quite a stir you've created with your pretty little nude outside." He gestured toward the gallery, then turned away from Eric's painting and began nosing around in a corner of the studio like a great black bear, flipping through stacks of canvases leaning against the wall. "You're sure to make all the papers. Quite a *succès de scandale*."

"They hung it without my permission."

"They always love you for your worst work, my boy. Better get used to it."

"I don't care what they like."

"They're so taken with her nubile contours,

they haven't noticed the meat hooks you've given her for hands. Haven't I taught you anything?" He returned to the new painting and asked Kitty which she preferred.

"This one," Kitty responded reluctantly, eyeing Mr. Westfield with suspicion.

"His *Hillbilly Laocoön?* Yes, very pretty, I agree."

"You hate it," Eric declared, the color leaving his cheeks.

"It's lovely," Kitty said, trying to bolster Eric's confidence.

"I think so, too," I added.

"And I should think you would," Mr. Westfield replied contemptuously. "Such passion in those quaint faces. Tolerable composition if we overlook the extremities."

If Kitty had not taken hold of Eric's right hand, he would have hurled the canvas to the floor, destroying it as he had the charcoal nude in life-drawing class. "Eric," she cried, "your mother's spirit lives in this painting. You must finish it."

"I hate it."

"Then do it for me, as my wedding gift."

"Isn't that a lovely idea," Westfield said mockingly.

"Sir," Kitty said, turning a cold eye upon him, "I don't know what it is my cousin sees in you, but I'll tell you what I see."

"Please do," he said, affecting indifference as

he clipped the end of a cigar. "I never tire of other people's opinions of me."

"You find yourself about to be eclipsed by a young man with more talent at the age of seventeen than you will ever have, and you are not only intensely jealous of him but doing everything in your power to undermine his confidence. I should have you reported."

Westfield struck a match and sucked deeply on his cigar, then said, "Go on."

"If you can't help my cousin, kindly leave him alone."

"Ah, the Hippocratic oath. Above all, do no harm. I quite agree. He has such a bright future ahead of him as the creator of pretty pictures. It would be a great pity to spoil so promising a career in the effort to get him to produce true art. You shall have your wedding painting. Please accept my sincerest congratulations."

I found myself completely baffled by him, unable to separate sincerity from deceit. Kitty, however, felt only anger. "Sir, are you a member of the faculty?"

"I am happy to report that I have been spared that fate. Other, more self-sacrificing individuals bear that onerous burden."

"Then you come here merely to torment the very students who admire you?"

"I have come today, dear lady, to pay homage to the work of your young cousin and to celebrate his newfound notoriety. Good day."

Mr. Westfield bowed to us and excused himself, saying he wanted to get one more look at Eric's "wonderfully unembellished portrait" before returning to his own insignificant work.

Kitty glared at him, muttering "buffoon" as he passed through the open door.

"Get out!" Eric growled at us.

"Don't listen to him," Kitty pleaded. "He's just jealous of you."

"Jealous? You don't know what you're talking about!" he cried. "Leave me alone. I didn't ask you to come here."

"Eric, please."

But before Kitty could say another word, he slammed his brushes down upon the easel and stormed out of the studio.

When I awoke the next morning it was raining. Kitty ordered breakfast in the room and ate silently, her face full of unspoken thoughts. When I asked if she felt all right, she said, "Fine. I just have a lot on my mind."

"Eric?" I hadn't been able to get him and Mr. Westfield out of my mind.

"He's the least of my worries."

"Are you nervous about getting married?"

"I suppose," she admitted. "It seemed so far away until this morning."

"Maybe you should wait a little longer. You haven't known Halvard all that long."

"You sound just like your father. I've waited thirty-one years. That's long enough."

I finished breakfast, then dressed for my walk to the library.

"Do you have to go?" she asked as I slipped on my coat.

I nodded.

"Take a cab then," she said, rising to get her purse.

"I'd rather walk," I insisted.

"If it's still raining, come back here for lunch. If not, I'll meet you there at twelve o'clock. You be careful now. Don't talk to strangers."

"I can take care of myself."

Kitty put her hand to her mouth in mock surprise. "If you aren't becoming your brother right before my eyes."

When I reached the street, I breathed deeply, glad to be on my own. The sidewalks were nearly empty. I pulled my coat collar shut and hurried uptown to the great marble library. Its broad white stairs glistened in the rain. Pigeons ambled about the covered terrace, cooing loudly from a dozen perches. Inside the cavernous entrance hall everything was white—the floor, the twin stairways, the columns, the vaulted ceiling—and all mutely lit by the half-light that passed through high, dusty windows. I asked a guard where old newspapers were kept and was directed down a long white corridor to a paneled room filled with heavy oak tables and chairs. Behind a bank teller's grating, a young woman sat reading.

"Can I help you?" she asked, closing her book as I approached.

"I'm looking for an old newspaper."

"We have lots of them." She smiled warmly. "Do you know which one?"

I shook my head.

"What is it, exactly, you want to know?"

"If my mother drowned," I blurted out.

"Excuse me?" she asked, studying me more carefully.

"My mother was on the *Holly Fair* when she sank. My brother said he read all about it in the newspapers."

"I'm so sorry," she said, her face full of pain. She pulled a large volume down from a shelf and began flipping through it rapidly, then said, "Here it is: *Holly Fair,* hearings on accidental drowning." She mentioned a date and the names of several newspapers, then looked through another book, wrote something down on a slip of paper, and told me she would be right back. I ran my fingers over the polished tables and the shiny lamp stands, feeling a sudden nervousness. Maybe Kitty was right. Perhaps it was better just to know my own heart. I looked toward the door but didn't move.

When the librarian returned, she carried an armful of newspapers. "You'll find the accident mentioned in all of these," she said, setting them down on one of the tables. "They're in chronological order. If you need more information, just ask." She laid her hand on my shoulder a moment, then returned to her seat behind the grate. I looked at the pile and shivered.

The first story appeared near the bottom of an inside page under a small black headline that read: "Steamer Sinks Moments After Launch."

The two-paragraph story described the collision but said nothing about drownings. For a moment my old hope revived—perhaps Mama hadn't died after all. I picked up the second paper. The headline was larger and at the top of the front page: "Three Drowned, Two Missing in *Holly Fair* Collision." The article ran to the bottom of the front page and continued inside with a photograph of the sunken ship, only the wheelhouse and smokestacks visible above the water. There I found Mama's name mentioned for the first time. I stared at it a long while, feeling something small and white take flight from my heart.

The other papers described the accident in greater detail, one naming the cemetery where Mama was buried, but none mentioned the missing child or the frantic mother. Toward the bottom of the pile I found a small story about a safety hearing concerning the accident and the ship's evacuation procedures. It was there that the captain reported, "We were well prepared for such an eventuality. The crew drilled regularly. The only loss of life resulted when a passenger deliberately disobeyed the instructions of my crew and refused to ascend to the lifeboat deck. We saved nearly three thousand lives that morning. I deeply regret the loss of my two crew members and that of the passenger, Mrs. Burns, but those fatalities were not the fault of procedure. The successful rescue of so many lives proves otherwise." The very last paper mentioned the utility closet where

Mama was found. But the testimony of the diver who removed her body indicated she probably took refuge there in the mistaken belief that it was watertight. The compartment beside her was.

After reading the reports, I stared through the dusty windows at the rain. If only the barge hadn't been passing at that moment; if only the captain had been able to get the ship back into port; if only Mama hadn't met that panicky mother, hadn't gone down to the lowest deck, hadn't run away from us; if only Pa had been able to control his temper; if only Eric hadn't been so contrary.

"Did you find what you wanted?" the librarian asked as I returned the papers to her.

"Where is Woodville Cemetery?" I asked, barely able to control the tremor in my voice.

"The elevated goes there," she said, writing directions on a slip of paper. "It's not that far, maybe thirty minutes." When I thanked her, she repeated how sorry she was. Tears sprang to my eyes. I tried to blink them back, then hurried from the room.

I stood under the great portico, watching the rain bubble on the steps. The city itself seemed in mourning. I had to find Mama's grave and say good-bye to her. I looked at the directions in my hand then returned inside and called the hotel, leaving a message for Kitty that I needed more time and would meet her for supper. When the rain let up briefly, I ran to the elevated station and climbed the steep iron steps to the tracks. The city was unusually quiet, only an occasional wagon or taxi passing beneath me. I waited fifteen minutes, watching the rain splash through the wooden ties to the street below. Just when I thought the train would never come, the rails began to hum. In the distance a steam engine rounded a curve between tall buildings and roared toward me, spewing smoke and steam, rattling the platform. With an ear-shattering squeal, the five empty cars slowed to a stop. I took a seat beside a large, rain-splattered window and spent the next half hour watching the city slip by, peering into hundreds of apartments. In one a woman was hanging sheets to dry, in another a man sat reading, in a third an elderly couple ate lunch. Children waved at the passing train, cats climbed along narrow windowsills, flowers fluttered in sooty window boxes. Gradually the scenery began to change. The tracks dropped to street level, the buildings stood farther apart. Trees appeared, a few at first, then whole stands of them. We stopped less frequently, traveling at greater speed, the rails clicking beneath the car like a vaudeville stage full of tap dancers.

By the time we arrived at the Woodville station, the rain had diminished to a cold drizzle. I stepped onto the platform and watched the train disappear, feeling suddenly abandoned. Except for a small cluster of shops—a florist, a stone carver, a grocery—there was nothing in Woodville but

the sprawling, silent cemetery. The main entrance, a huge cast-iron gate with the words
"Woodville Cemetery" inscribed at the top, stood
at the base of a sparsely wooded hill within sight
of the train. Just inside the fence, hundreds of
gray tombstones followed the contours of the hill,
separated by flowering shrubs and trees.

I passed through the gate and began walking
among the weathered stones, wondering how
each person had died: the old woman born in
Greece a hundred and ten years ago, the twenty-
year-old man with the same first and last name,
the five infants buried side by side. I wondered,
too, how I would ever find Mama's grave in so
vast a place. Halfway up the hill I came upon a
gardener, a short, bearded man who hummed to
himself in rhythm with his rapidly clicking prun-
ing shears. When I asked him how to locate Mama's grave, he pointed toward a stone building
near the main gate.

Inside, a pinched, angry-eyed woman greeted
me with suspicion, asking impatiently what I
wanted.

"To see my mother's grave," I said.

"The grounds are open till five," she replied
sharply.

"I don't know where she's buried."

"What's her name?" she asked with annoyance.

"Margaret Burns."

"Spell it."

I did.

"Date of death?"

"A year ago."

"Exact date," she snapped, then thumbed through a thick register lying open before her. "Section twenty-seven, row nine, plot fourteen," she said. I leaned over the desk and followed her finger. There, in the precise script of a book-keeper, was Mama's name in black ink. The woman scowled at me for looking at her book and quickly turned to a blank page.

"Where is that?" I asked.

She exhaled deeply, opened a drawer, and withdrew a small map. "There," she spat, pointing to a nearly invisible rectangle amid thousands of others.

"How do I get there?" I asked meekly.

She shook her head in annoyance and ran her finger along a thick black line leading from the office to the farthest corner of the cemetery. "Just look for the section marker."

At that moment a tall, clean-shaven man in a shiny black suit entered and dropped into a chair beside the woman's desk. "So how'd it go?" she asked him, breaking into a broad grin.

"You should have seen the look on her face," the man said, stretching his long legs before him. He removed a cigar from his pocket, bit off the end, and lit it. I listened to their conversation for several minutes, wondering what they both found so amusing, then interrupted to ask once more where Mama was buried.

"Didn't anyone ever teach you no manners?" the woman scowled.

"What's the kid want?" the man asked.

"Mother's up in twenty-seven."

"I've got a delivery that way. Want a ride, kid?"

"Yes, please," I said with relief.

"No problem." Then he continued talking to the woman until his cigar was nothing but a stub of white ash. I waited with growing impatience, staring out the window at the hill of graves, watching the drizzle turn back to rain.

Finally the man rose from his chair. "Ready, kid?" he asked, stepping outside. I had to run to keep up with him as he walked toward a black truck parked a short way up the hill.

"Want to ride in front or back?" he asked with a grin. The rear of the truck was open and covered with flowers. "You've got time yet before you have to ride back there," he declared before I could answer. "That one there was eighty-eight. Tough old bird. Outlasted her whole family. Nobody left to see her off. Hop in."

I realized then that the flowers covered a coffin; the truck was a hearse. He started the noisy engine, threw it into gear, and began climbing the steep hill, waving at the gardener. The rain fell hard, blotting the windshield. At the top we looked out over open fields strewn with grave-stones. "Pretty sight, eh. Got me a little place all reserved." He pointed toward a half-empty hill-side. "Place is filling up fast. Never hurts to be prepared."

The hearse backfired as we headed downhill, then sputtered and coughed during the next climb. Near the top the driver rolled to a stop and pointed off to the right side. "That's twenty-seven. You know the row?"

"I forgot." Section twenty-seven looked differ-ent from the others, more open.

"She's in there somewhere. You can read, can't you?"

"Yes, sir."

"Check the markers. You'll find her."

Two men dressed in long black raincoats and hats stood up to their necks in a hole while a third watched. The driver called them over, shook their muddy hands, then handed them each a cigar. Together they carried the coffin to the open grave, tilted it sharply, and let it slide to the bot-tom where it landed with a crack. Then they stood under a broad oak, smoking and laughing.

I entered section twenty-seven and began look-ing for Mama's grave. What made it look differ-ent was the absence of fancy tombstones. Every grave was marked with a small gray footstone half hidden by grass. I walked the rows, reading each name, my heart fluttering every time I came upon one beginning with an *M* or a *B*. And then

I found it, a flat stone like all the others, the grass growing over the edges, Mama's name and the date she died partially covered with dirt and leaves. I dropped to my knees and brushed away the debris, muttering, "Mama, Mama." With the end of a stick, I cleaned out the deeply carved letters of her name, then pulled up the grass and weeds.

"I'm here, Mama," I whispered, laying my forehead against the cold, wet stone. "I've missed you so much. Why did you have to die?"

I could feel her there, just out of reach. I knew she was listening, so I told her about Eric running away to the city and Kitty coming to live with us, about Pa's leg getting worse and Halvard's marriage proposal, about the newspaper accounts of the accident and the little boy who was never really lost. "I know you didn't mean to drown," I whispered. "You were coming home."

Then for a long while I just knelt in the wet grass listening to the rain until the dampness began to seep through my coat.

"I'll never forget you, Mama," I whispered, kissing the stone one last time.

CHAPTER

19

I didn't mention the cemetery when I returned to the hotel. Kitty was so engrossed in a newspaper story about the academy art show that she forgot to ask about my visit to the library. "Your brother is famous!" she cried as I entered the room. "Look!" Filling the center of an inside page was a long review of the Academy show. The first painting mentioned was "*Lisa* by the talented seventeen-year-old art student Eric Berns."

"They spelled our name wrong," I said.

"Did they?" she asked rereading the story. "I was so excited, I didn't notice. Listen to what they said."

She ran her finger down the column of black print, then raised the paper from the sofa and read, "The most exciting discovery of the show, however, was that of the promising young student Eric Berns. As we wandered about the gallery eliciting responses to his striking life-size nude,

Lisa, the word *astonishing* was frequently invoked. And with good reason, for it is nothing short of astonishing when a mere boy of seventeen exhibits such control of the fundamentals of human anatomy, even more astonishing when he displays such insight into the more rarefied realms of human nature. Lisa glares forth with an imperiousness that defies censure, her beauty subordinated by her strength of will. So powerful is her gaze that one almost overlooks the few minor technical flaws of perspective in the artist's execution. These will undoubtedly be overcome as the gifted young artist matures. Indeed, what he lacks is precisely what such schools as the Art Academy are able to provide. What he excels at, portraiture of the human soul, no school can impart. In Eric Berns the city has found an exciting new talent with a startling vision for our times."

Kitty let out a little scream of excitement and dropped the paper to her lap. "Isn't that wonderful!"

"Let me see it," I said, taking the paper from her. The writer was not at all complimentary in covering the rest of the show, calling the other paintings "bloodless, derivative, and uninspired."

"Come," Kitty said, throwing her shawl over her shoulders and reaching for an umbrella. "We'll get a bite to eat downstairs and then congratulate Eric on his success."

Half an hour later we were hurrying through the rain to the academy. The exhibition gallery was open but nearly empty except for six well-dressed women standing at the far end of the room repeating the words they had read in the morning paper. "She *is* regal, isn't she," one said. "Very proud," another responded. Kitty inched closer and when she could no longer restrain herself asked me in a too-loud voice, "What do you think of your brother's work?"

The women turned our way. One, wearing a fur collar, asked with a haughty air, "Is your brother Eric Burns?"

"This is Nathan Burns," Kitty replied, "Eric's younger brother."

"I wonder what your mother thinks of his painting such pictures," the woman said with a look of disgust. "Personally, I find it quite shocking."

"Now, Gladys, don't be so old-fashioned," another of the group remarked. "Times are changing."

"Then I quite prefer the old, thank you."

Kitty puffed herself up proudly and said, "I'm sure his mother would be very proud of his work if she were alive to see it."

"Oh, I'm sorry," the kinder lady replied. But the lady in the fur collar said only, "No wonder," and moved on to the other paintings, followed by her friends.

Kitty and I studied Eric's portrait another moment, then we crossed the rain-soaked courtyard and asked the first passing student if he had seen Eric. "You mean 'the exciting new talent with a startling vision for our times?'" he replied sarcastically, and hurried away. Kitty looked at me with surprise and turned to another student who replied, "He's probably lunching with the mayor."

When we reached the painting studio, we found a handful of students working on their canvases. They looked up a moment as we entered, then resumed painting. We walked to the back of the room and found Eric's painting covered by a dirty sheet.

"Shall we peek?" Kitty asked.

As she began to lift the sheet, a deep voice bellowed, "Can I help you?"

It was Mr. Westfield, standing half hidden by a huge canvas, a white, paint-smeared smock over his vest, several paintbrushes in his left hand.

"Mr. Westfield? I thought you said you were not a member of the faculty," Kitty replied.

"I am merely a guest here," he said. "They refer to me as 'artist in residence,' as though I were a part of the edifice."

"Is my cousin here?"

"Probably off celebrating his newfound fame."

"We've come for a last look before returning home," she explained, indicating Eric's canvas.

"Back to the land of nubile maidens?"

"Why do you insist upon mocking us?" Kitty asked, facing him squarely. "Do you assume just because we come from the country that we are too ignorant to know when we are being ridiculed?"

"Quite the contrary," he replied. "I assume that you are so self-sufficient as to have little need of us city dwellers and our idle artistic pursuits. You are the salt of the earth, the true laborers in the vineyards of the Lord. What we do here is but a specter, a pale imitation of the real life you lead."

"Then why do you sound so contemptuous?"

"Do I? Forgive me. Force of habit. In truth, I envy you your closeness to nature, your innate understanding of the rhythms of life, your simple perfection. I envy your daily tasks, your well-earned rest."

"We are no simpler than you, sir. And our rest is just as troubled as yours. Eric is certainly proof of that."

"Eric is not nearly as complicated as you imagine," he said. "He is driven by anger. It feeds his work. The angrier he becomes, the harder he labors. The moment he grows satisfied with himself or his painting, he will cease to create. And that would be a great pity, for he has a keen eye and a prodigious memory, and will, under the proper conditions, develop quite an original vision, not this salon portraiture he's exploring just now but something wholly new, perhaps revolutionary. He will not be content to paint in conventional styles for very long. He will need to carve out his own territory to achieve true art, provided all this premature notoriety doesn't interfere. An early success is too often fatal, robbing an artist of his essential uncertainty."

"Eric is stronger than that. He doesn't care what others think. He never has."

"Then he won't be harmed by my efforts to counterbalance all that thoughtless adulation," Mr. Westfield said with sudden and surprising softness.

"No, I suppose not," she admitted.

Mr. Westfield set aside his brushes, then, as carefully as a father lifts the veil from his daughter's face, he removed the sheet from Eric's canvas. The three figures in the foreground had changed only slightly, but Pa's leg had been repainted and the decaying cabin had come into startling relief with its splintered boards and exposed nails. Eric had added a spot of white as well—Bianca, caught at the moment of leaping from the porch roof.

"He's made considerable progress since yesterday," Mr. Westfield observed. "It was in danger of becoming quite commonplace. But in his anger he has begun to forge a new icon. Praise him if you must, but don't rob him of his creative wellspring."

"Are you saying he has to choose between happiness and creativity?"

"I prefer to say the choice is between contentment and creativity. I've yet to meet a contented pioneer in any field. Creativity is spawned by a deep dissatisfaction with life."

"I don't believe that," Kitty challenged.

"You would term the creative process, perhaps, a sanctification, an expression of gratitude, the artist's prayer offering." Something of his former scorn began to creep back into his voice.

"Yes, I would," she declared.

"Believe what you must, but don't encourage Eric to accept anything less than the perfection he is capable of."

A student called Mr. Westfield across the room. We stood before Eric's painting for several minutes, then Kitty carefully lowered the sheet and suggested we try his apartment. We did not find him there but down the street washing dishes in the restaurant where he worked twice a week, an apron tied around his waist.

"Can you have dinner with us?" Kitty asked.

"I ate already," he replied, his arms deep in soapy water.

"Mr. Westfield said you worked all night. Have you slept?"

"During my lunch break."

"Did you see that wonderful article in this morning's paper?" Kitty asked full of excitement.

"I never read the paper."

"You're famous," I said proudly.

"You ought to be celebrating," Kitty added.

"I bet you could sell it for a lot of money," I said.

"And not have to wash dishes," Kitty remarked.

"I like washing dishes," he declared.

Kitty laughed. "I wish I'd known that back home. Will you, at least, join us for coffee? It's our last night. We want to celebrate your success."

"There's nothing to celebrate," he said, slapping more dishes into the water. "They don't know what they're talking about. Every year they single out one student and make all the others look like fools. The only fool is that stupid critic."

"I thought his article was very perceptive," Kitty said.

"He doesn't know the first thing about painting."

"Well, I guess I don't either. But I think your portrait is wonderful and so does Mr. Westfield."

"No, he doesn't. He thinks I'm a dumb hillbilly."

"That's just his way of keeping you humble," Kitty explained.

Eric lifted a rack of dishes to his chest and carried it out to the dining room. When he didn't return, we peeked through the curtain into the front of the restaurant. Eric stood carefully folding napkins into flowers that he set in the center of each freshly washed plate. He worked quickly, transforming the limp linen into blossoms that seemed to grow out of the white china.

"How about that coffee?" Kitty tried again.

"Can't," he said without offering an explanation.

"We sail tomorrow morning at ten," Kitty told him. "Will you be able to see us off?"

"I've got a class at nine."

"Breakfast, then?"

He shook his head.

"Then I guess this is good-bye," she said, trying to conceal her disappointment.

"I guess so," he replied without turning around.

Kitty looked at me, her eyes full of pain. "I hope I live to see the day I understand you Burns men."

CHAPTER

20

☙ We boarded the *New Hope* the next morning, our trunk and grip supplemented by two
dozen cardboard boxes bound tightly with twine.
Until the last moment Kitty hoped Eric would
join us for breakfast or at least see us off at the
pier, but he did neither. As the ten o'clock whistle
sounded and the great paddle wheel churned into
motion, we stood at the rail, taking a last long
look at the city. It no longer felt so foreign. I had
begun to understand something of its strange
ways, enough to know that Eric belonged there
and I didn't. The city was intended for people
like him, people seething with angry energy, or
people like Kitty, full of high spirits and a skin
thick enough to withstand the daily shocks the
city inflicted on everyone who walked its
crowded, noisy streets.

The next morning Pa was waiting for us at
the pier. I ran down the gangway, the planks

bouncing beneath me, glad to be back. Pa climbed down from the wagon with difficulty, the muscles in his neck as tense as woven hemp. He held on to the side as he came around to help me lift the trunk into the back, hardly putting any weight on his bad leg, his eyes dark with pain.

"Is it so bad?" Kitty asked with concern.

"It's always bad," Pa groaned.

"You ought to have a doctor look at it."

"So he can tell me it's lame? I know that already." He climbed back in the wagon, waited for us to join him, then clucked at Dart.

"Sometimes doctors can help."

"There's no help for this but a hacksaw."

We left the river, heading slowly toward Providence.

"How's Zeke?" I asked.

"Took off yesterday to look at some fancy new breed of sheep upriver. He'll be back tomorrow."

"I'm sorry you didn't join us," Kitty said after a moment. "We had a wonderful time."

"You might have saved yourself the trouble," Pa replied ominously.

"What do you mean?"

"The wedding's off."

"What are you talking about, Uncle Ray?"

"Just what I said. Hejdling came by yesterday and told me his boy had changed his mind. Didn't offer any explanations, just threw a copy of the newspaper down on the table and left."

"Eric's painting?" Kitty asked, her hand over her mouth.

"Painting? More like obscenity." Pa's fists clenched the reins, knotting the muscles in his forearms. "They do him a kindness and he repays them with a slap in the face."

"He didn't mean it as an insult."

"Don't tell me what he *meant*. Anyone with two eyes can see clear enough what he meant. That boy won't be happy till he heaps shame on us all."

"It's really very beautiful," Kitty tried to explain.

"Didn't you hear what I said? Your wedding's been scuttled on account of that painting. You still want to defend it? Save your breath for Hejdling."

"Did Halvard say anything?"

"I told you, I only saw his father."

"Then the wedding's not off," Kitty said defiantly.

"How do you figure that?"

"Halvard makes his own decisions, not his father."

"You think that little peacock's gonna cross his father on something like this? No, ma'am. If Hejdling says it's off, it's off."

Kitty said nothing more until we neared home, then asked Pa to let her off as we passed the Hejdlings' drive.

"You're wasting your time," Pa insisted, stopping the wagon.

"No, I'm not, Uncle Ray. I'm saving my life."

I turned and watched her walk toward their house as we climbed the hill toward home. "You ready to get back to work?" Pa asked. "Or have you taken it into your head to run off, too?" A hint of desperation mingled with his usual anger.

"I'm staying, Pa," I said.

"Can't see how anybody stands it down there," he said more gently. "Your mother had a taste for it, but she belonged up here and she knew it." It was the first time he had mentioned her without anger.

"I found where she's buried," I said.

"Is it a nice spot?" he asked.

"It's on a hillside full of trees and flowers."

"She'd like that." He laid his hand on my knee.

When we reached the house, Rebel bounded down from the barn, running between the wheels of the wagon. "That lamb's gonna come to grief before he's big enough to eat," Pa snapped.

"You're not gonna butcher him, are you?" I asked.

"No, I suppose not," he conceded. "Hardly worth the trouble. Bottle-fed lambs never bulk out."

"He could replace the ram we lost to the mountain lion."

"This little runt?" He laughed. "Well, we'll see."

Hunter rose from the shade and ambled over to be petted. A pair of newborn calico kittens, their spotted brown faces no larger than the circle made by my thumb and forefinger, poked out from between freshly split firewood.

"When were they born?" I asked.

"Day after you left. Three lambs, too, and one of the mares is about to foal. We've got our hands full."

He climbed down slowly and took hold of the trunk, but as we stepped away from the wagon he tripped over a rock and crumpled to the ground as though someone had pulled a pin out of his leg. His face turned ashen; sweat beaded on his forehead. He tried to stand but could not maneuver his bad leg under him.

"What's the matter, Pa?" I cried.

"Give me a hand," he groaned. I knelt down and draped his arm around my shoulder, then slowly rose, his full weight bearing down on my back. "Just get me to the doorway," he panted, hopping and wincing, his bad leg dragging uselessly behind. We paused at the woodpile, then again by the door, his body twisting awkwardly with each step. When we got inside he collapsed onto the parlor sofa and shut his eyes, breathing heavily.

"Should I get the doctor?"

"Just get me some water," he whispered through cracked lips.

I ran to the kitchen for a cup.

"Here, Pa," I said, standing over him. He seemed not to hear, lost in his agony. After a long moment his eyes focused on me.

"You're a good boy," he whispered, sipping from the cup as I held it to his lips. He ran his palm over my head, then let his arm drop heavily to the sofa.

Toward evening, as I walked the newly planted corn rows, Halvard and Kitty drove up to the house. He did not hand her down as usual, just stopped long enough for her to climb out before turning the wagon sharply and trotting back out to the road. Kitty watched him go, then walked slowly toward me. The sheep had begun to gather for their twilight vigil at the top of the pasture, brass collar bells clinking as they hurried through the thick grass, the low-lying sun spreading a blanket of pink light over the fields.

Kitty watched them, her face thick with thought. I joined her by the stone wall, stepping over the corn rows, the soft earth giving way beneath my bare feet.

"Pa's leg's real bad," I said.

She didn't respond. Halvard's carriage had come into view across the valley, trotting up to his barn.

"They don't understand," she said, more to herself than to me. "Halvard's trying. He never had anything against Eric. But it's difficult with his father so set against him. Lisa can't leave the farm without getting smirked at. People are saying the worst things about her and Eric. His father wouldn't even see me."

"What's gonna happen?"

"Don't know." She reached absentmindedly into her skirt pocket and pulled out a flat green stone polished smooth by water. "Bittle was sweet, though—gave me this." She turned it over in her fingers, a faint smile returning to her lips. Then, casting off her despondency, she asked, "What's that you said about Uncle Ray's leg?"

"He can't put any weight on it."

"We better go see what we can do."

We found Pa where I had left him, lying sprawled across the sofa, sleeping fitfully, his forehead damp with sweat. I couldn't remember ever seeing him doze off like that before supper.

Kitty tied on her apron, rolled up her sleeves, and lit the stove. When Pa awoke she asked, "Why didn't you wire us?"

"It's gone lame on me before. I'll be all right." His voice was chiseled thin by suffering.

Kitty brought his dinner into the parlor, but he hardly touched it. Just sitting up made him wince with pain.

"You're sleeping right here tonight," Kitty insisted. "And tomorrow the doctor's gonna take a look at that leg."

Pa frowned but didn't object, falling back

breathless against the pillows. His skin looked yellow; his face white. *This is how he will look when he dies,* I thought, feeling my chest tighten.

I knelt beside the sofa and asked, "What can I do, Pa?" He laid his hand on my shoulder.

"You and Zeke gotta cultivate the wheat tomorrow," he said, his voice little more than a whisper, his eyes closed. "The weeds are setting. Meant to get to it all week."

"Okay."

"And the upper pasture needs mowing."

"We'll do that, too."

"Get some rest."

When I rose he opened his eyes a moment. They were glassy with pain. "You're too young to be taking care of your pa."

"I don't mind."

When I turned to go he asked weakly, "What did you think of your brother's painting?"

"Everybody says he's got real talent."

"You don't think he's wasting his time?"

"Nope."

"I guess he's old enough to know his own mind."

At dawn I slipped out of bed and down to the kitchen, put the kettle up, then stepped outside for more firewood. The sky was a transparent blue, the air already alive with honeybees and songbirds. Bianca fluttered down to the woodpile. I walked up to the barn and threw open the doors, releasing the night's cold, stale air, then fed and watered the horses, spread fresh hay for the lambs, let the sheep out, and milked the goats. When I got back to the house, Kitty was just entering the kitchen, her hair uncombed, her collar misbuttoned.

"How'd you sleep?" she asked.

"Okay. You look tired."

"Never tell a woman that, even if it's true." She studied her reflection in the bottom of a copper pan. "I'm not used to all this silence after a week in the city."

It isn't the silence, but Halvard, I thought.

She looked back at me a moment, as though she heard my thought, then started breakfast, setting my plate down in Pa's place at the head of the table. I ate quickly, anxious to begin the cultivating.

"Why don't you wait for Zeke?" she asked.

"He might not get back till late. There's too much to do."

"Well, you do a man's work, you eat a man's breakfast," she insisted, pointing to my unfinished eggs. After I'd cleaned my plate, she warned, "You take your time out there. That field doesn't have to be finished in one day. You've got the whole summer and a lifetime of summers after that. Slow and steady, that's what counts."

I hitched Doc and Dart to the cultivator, climbed onto the metal seat, and headed for the wheat field. The sun was warm on my back.

Midmorning I shed my shirt and donned one of Pa's old straw hats. When Kitty brought out lunch, we sat together on the wall.

"How's Pa?" I asked.

"Hardly touched his breakfast. Wanted to know how you were making out."

"What did you tell him?"

"That he didn't need to ask. The doctor's looking at him now."

I felt relieved.

"Any sign of Zeke?" I wanted him back but not before I had shown Pa how much I could do on my own.

"Seems he's decided to make a grand tour of the region. He sent word this morning of another farm he wants to visit, says he's doing a 'scientific' study of all the new breeds. Might be gone a week or more."

I smiled.

"Now don't start getting all Burns independent on me," she scolded.

I finished my lunch and slipped off the wall.

"You won't be any good tomorrow if you don't take it easy today," Kitty insisted.

"I spent all last week taking it easy."

"I should know better than to come between a Burns and his field, or his canvas, for that matter."

As I rode the long rows in the heat, my mind drifted off to thoughts of what it would be like when the farm was mine. I'd marry Sonja. We'd add a few cows to the place, clear the land around the cabin, and put it to the plow. I had my whole life before me, as Kitty said. I would plant my dreams in that soil and watch them grow.

Late afternoon, Kitty returned with a jug of ice water, the sweetest I'd ever tasted. My arms and shoulders had begun to ache, but I only noticed the pain when I stopped.

"What did the doc say about Pa?" I asked.

"That if he wasn't so stubborn and thick skulled, he could have spared himself a lot of pain."

"Is he gonna be all right?"

"His hip's terribly inflamed. Drove himself too hard while we were away. He's got to stay off it for a month or he might never walk again."

"A month!"

"That's just the way Uncle Ray took it."

"He'll never listen."

"He's got no choice."

I finished the last row of wheat as the sun slipped behind the Hejdlings' ridge. Bone weary, I felt like lying down right there in the middle of the field and sleeping until morning, but there was still so much to do. *How had Pa managed alone all these years,* I wondered. At the barn I unhitched and watered the horses, resting my face against their warm flanks as I wiped the sweat from their dusty coats. I fed the goats and counted the sheep, noticing that one restive ewe kept circling the barn, looking for a comfortable, remote corner to bed down in, her guttural bleats full of pain. Through the fog of my exhaustion, I thought, *She's gonna birth anytime now,* then stumbled back to the house wanting nothing more than to collapse on the sofa for a few minutes before supper.

I never ate that night. I vaguely remember Kitty telling me to wash up and my mumbling something about needing a minute or two to catch my breath. Then someone was shaking me by the shoulder, whispering, "Get up, Nathan, wake up."

"I'm coming," I muttered, rolling over. But the voice kept insisting, and the hand continued to rock my shoulder until sleep dissolved and my eyes opened to a flickering candle. Kitty stood beside me in a bathrobe, her hair awry, the muted bleating of a ewe coming from the barn.

"We've got to help her," she said. "It's been two hours already. Uncle Ray tried to get down the stairs and nearly broke his neck. Says it's her first lamb."

She grabbed my legs and set them on the floor, then pulled me upright. My head swam, my stomach grew queasy. I wanted desperately to lie back and close my eyes.

"Don't fall asleep on me," she said, forcing me to drink a cup of hot coffee.

"What time is it?" I mumbled.

"Little past midnight."

She helped me to my feet. My mind began to

clear. I could hear the ewe now. Pa called me into the parlor. He was half sitting, half lying on the sofa, his overalls unstrapped.

"You know what to do?" he asked. I shook my head. He explained how to help birth the lamb and reminded me to take along a bottle of goat's milk. "She's probably just fighting it, more scared than anything," he said.

We found the groaning ewe lying on her side in bloody straw. Every few minutes she panted and pushed. The crown of her lamb's head would appear between her hind legs, only to disappear again as soon as the contraction subsided.

"Cord must be wrapped around the neck," Kitty said, holding the kitchen lamp over the ewe.

"What should we do?" I asked.

"Free it."

"How?"

"I don't know."

Another powerful spasm overtook the ewe. Kitty stroked her head. When the spasm passed I reached inside the ewe until I could feel the wiry lamb's head and the small snout. My fingers searched for the neck and found the warm, eel-like umbilical cord pulsing rapidly. It was wrapped twice around the narrow neck.

The ewe began to push again, jamming the lamb against my fingers. I withdrew quickly and waited, then reached in once more, working rapidly, looping the cord once, then twice over the head. The contractions began again and this time the head popped into the light. I eased the shoulders and forelegs forward, then let the ewe complete the job with a powerful thrust that dropped the lamb into my blood-soaked hands. The mother's head collapsed into the straw, her chest heaving with exhaustion.

"It's all over," I said, showing her the lamb. She sniffed at it, then began to clean it with her tongue. After several minutes I wrapped the wet lamb in a towel, lay it across my lap, and began to feed it from Rebel's old baby bottle. The little ewe drank hungrily, then curled up next to her mother and fell asleep.

"Nathan Burns," Kitty whispered with a grin, "you're a natural."

CHAPTER

21

Pa was lying on the sofa when I came down the next morning, an open letter at his elbow. He looked weary but in less pain. Kitty was up in the barn milking the goats and tending to my chores. The sun was already high, the air thick and warm.

"Sorry I overslept," I apologized.

"Kitty says you saved the ewe and her lamb last night," Pa said, his voice just above a whisper.

"Only had to untangle 'em."

"I guess that about makes up for our losses last winter. Go get your breakfast."

I poured myself a cup of weak coffee with plenty of milk, then returned to the parlor. Pa's bad leg lay out to the side, the knee stiff, his foot shoeless.

"That from Eric?" I asked boldly, pointing to the letter. I didn't feel my usual fear of Pa's anger.

"Halvard," he replied.

"About Kitty?"

Pa nodded. "He wants to 'reimburse' us for all Kitty's wedding expenses." He threw the letter on the coffee table in disgust.

"Does Kitty know?"

"Yup."

"Then the wedding's off?"

"Seems so."

"Just because of Eric's painting?"

"That, and maybe Kitty not wanting to live with them over there, and their not caring to be any closer connected to this family than necessary."

"Do you blame them, Pa?"

"I think a man's word is more important than some damn fool picture."

Kitty kept to herself the next few days, fixing our meals but not sitting down to eat with us. She said she had no appetite. When I told her I was sorry about what happened between her and Halvard, she just shook her head.

Zeke returned at the end of the week, full of plans to enlarge our herd with a new breed from Australia that he said produced twice as much wool as our sheep and a higher quality mutton.

"I'll stick with what I know and can afford," Pa snorted over dinner.

"What do you think, Nate?" Zeke asked me.

I was surprised to be asked.

"I don't know," I replied, glancing at Pa.

"Time you had an opinion," Pa said. "This farm's fast becoming more yours than mine."

The idea stunned me. Kitty always said I'd be the first twelve-year-old to run my own farm. I wasn't running it, exactly, but I *was* doing an awful lot of the work. It was good to have Zeke back.

"I'll fill you in," Zeke said, his face bright with new plans. "I spy an opportunity here, one that could make a big difference in the future. We clear a bit more pasture, plant a few more acres, we could double our operation."

"And your labor," Pa reminded him. "You boys go slow. The difference between opportunity and undoing is careful planning—and luck."

Nothing more was said about Kitty and Halvard. With the coming of summer we were all too busy to dwell on it. While Pa slowly recovered, Zeke and I saw to his chores, Kitty to mine. The third week of June we began mowing the pastures, cutting the tall grass with the mechanical scythe, then turning it over by hand. Pa always said haying was the sweetest work on the farm. It filled the air with the delicious aroma of freshly cut grass. Kitty brought out our lunch and we ate and napped in the shade of the sugar maples, using a heap of hay cuttings for a pillow. No sleep ever felt as sweet.

That same week I prepared Kitty's kitchen

garden, turning over half an acre beyond the clothesline. She planted it with salad greens and herbs, tomatoes, cabbage, sweet corn, and flowers, working harder than ever but without her usual cheerfulness. Mealtime she just picked at her food, rising after a few bites to wash out pots and pans or to knead dough for the next day's bread. Her skirts and dresses began to hang on her.

"Seems to me you're losing flesh," Zeke remarked one night.

"Nothing wrong with a body shedding a little extra ballast when the weather turns warm," Kitty replied. "You want to know where all that flesh has gone, just look there." She pointed at me. "His pants hardly cover his shins."

She held a plate of potatoes out, and when I reached for them my shirt sleeve cinched halfway up my arm. "Look at that. He's growing out of clothes faster than I can sew them."

"Doing man's work grows a boy faster than anything I know," Pa said.

Pa kept to the house most of June, taking small, cautious steps, leaning on the backs of chairs as he moved from his desk to the kitchen to the sofa. After three weeks he ventured up to the barn with the help of a crutch. Sitting on an old crate, he mended the harness Eric had torn, then began oiling and overhauling all the other farm machinery. Hunter kept him company, bedding down in a cool corner of the tack room.

In July Zeke and I hauled the plank table up from the vegetable cellar so we could eat supper under the trees. Pa turned his attention to the neglected hives, cleaning out the dead drones and rebuilding the frames. We harvested more honey that year than in the previous two combined.

The August drought came on hard, one blistering, rainless day following another for almost three weeks, cracking the parched earth, burning the pasture grass. Just as the crops began to show signs of withering, the rains returned, breaking the heat and saturating the soil. We needed the rest as much as the crops needed the water and spent those three wet days lying about the house as though it were midwinter, grateful for the release from routine. When the sun returned, the grass shot up another foot and the corn tasseled. Then came the slow, dreamy days of late August, full of shimmering afternoon heat and great white thunderheads. The corncobs released their silk, the tomatoes grew heavy on the vine, the sheep fattened on the rich green grass.

Mornings, before it got too hot, Zeke and I mended fences and split firewood, talking about the future. He'd taken out a subscription to a sheepherders journal that was filled with new "scientific" ideas every month, and he was considering enrolling in the state agricultural college. I began reading the journals after he was done with them.

On the hottest afternoons I swam in the pond

and wandered the woods gathering berries. At sunset I climbed to the old cabin and looked off into the August haze, listening to the rumble of distant thunder. It was the time of year Mama had loved best, when the heat brought everything to a standstill—the sheep lying in the shade of the maples, the horses seeking the cool of the woods, Hunter asleep beneath the picnic table, even Pa at rest, lying in the hammock—nothing stirring but the cicadas and the spiraling hawks.

One evening after supper, as we sat watching the stars come out, Kitty mused, "When I was a girl, we used to have our village picnic this time of year." She smiled for the first time in months. "The whole town came. Folks brought their favorite salads and pies. At night there was always a huge bonfire."

"Sounds like fun to me," Zeke said.

"No one's likely to include us, not after what Eric did," Pa reflected ruefully.

"Then we'll do the inviting," Kitty declared.

"They wouldn't come."

"The prospect of good food has a way of overcoming even the most rigid scruples," Kitty insisted.

"Not among the Hejdlings."

"They're not our only neighbors."

"Could we have a bonfire?" I asked.

"Wouldn't be a proper picnic without one."

Pa shot us both a look of disbelief. "Isn't their

contempt obvious enough without inviting them to spit in our faces?"

"I'm willing to take that chance. If I'm gonna spend the rest of my life on this godforsaken ridge, there will have to be some changes. I'm tired of living like a hermit. I bear no grudges. Maybe I wasn't meant to marry, but that doesn't mean I've got to stay locked away up here."

"No, it doesn't," Zeke agreed. "There are plenty of nice folks in this town."

And you and Kitty could get married one day, I thought.

"Do as you like," Pa said, making it clear he'd take no part.

The next day Kitty and I drove through town calling on all our neighbors, inviting them to join us for a picnic the following Saturday. Most of them received us with an air of suspicion that quickly gave way to offers of assistance as soon as we told them of our plans. On the way home, we stopped at the Hejdlings' farm but went no farther than Gregory and Trudy's front porch at the bottom of the hill.

"I'd certainly love to join you," Trudy said cautiously, scanning the upper farm for signs of her father-in-law, "but you know how they are up the hill."

"You just tell them the whole town'll be there, and if they don't want to be thought unsociable, they better put in an appearance," Kitty said brightly.

Trudy promised to do what she could and offered to bring two cherry-rhubarb pies, then took Kitty's hand and whispered, "I think it's wrong what they done. Their quarrel's with Eric, not you."

Kitty's eyes welled up.

"I see Halvard looking off your way all the time," Trudy continued. "Gregory says he spends more time daydreaming than Bittle does. Everything we say to him we've got to say twice. You're never out of his thoughts."

Kitty squeezed her hand in gratitude, then said softly, "Even if they won't come, you try to slip away for an hour or two."

I added, "And tell Bittle we're gonna have the biggest bonfire he ever saw."

"I'll do that," Trudy said, releasing Kitty's hand.

Kitty devoted all that week to cooking and baking, preparing great vats of potato salad, shredded cabbage in vinegar, cucumbers in brine. She pulled up everything edible from the root cellar and threw it into the pot. When Pa complained we'd go hungry feeding half the county, she said, "We've got to make room for the new crops." Zeke and I carried out the last two bushels of apples, and all Friday afternoon we skinned and cored them in the shade of the orchard while Kitty rolled out the dough on the picnic table and put up a dozen pies.

Pa spent the week moving slowly around the house, making the kind of repairs Mama had been after him to do for years: replacing broken windows, scraping and painting doors, righting crooked shutters, resetting the stones lining the front path.

"If I didn't know better," Kitty said, watching him nail a new board on the privy roof, "I'd say Uncle Ray's looking forward to our little party."

"I plan to endure it," Pa muttered.

"Going to a heap of trouble for people you plan merely to endure," Zeke replied.

"I don't see any point in their going home gossiping that we can't keep after the place."

"Uncle Ray! When did you start caring what other people think?"

"I don't care. I'm thinking of you."

"Well, I'm mighty obliged," Kitty said, winking at me.

CHAPTER

22

❧ That Friday night was so hot and still, I slept on the picnic table with Hunter for company. Insects hummed in the grass and trees; the stars flickered weakly in the hazy air; the horses and sheep stirred restlessly. I drifted off for a few hours, then awoke feeling sticky and damp, a waning moon shedding a meager gray light across the orchard. Toward morning the air began to cool; the crickets ceased their chirping. A thin, white mist clung to the ground. I wrapped a blanket around me and walked through the wet grass. The tomatoes had begun to redden; the pumpkins were shading over from green to orange. Along the fringes of the woods, lone sugar maples had taken on the first colors of autumn.

When I returned to the house, Kitty was already preparing for our guests, washing plates and cups, slicing vegetables, setting pots to boil. "Did you scythe the grass under the apple trees?" she asked.

'Not yet."

"Readied extra feed for all the horses?"

"Nope."

"Brought down the planks and sawhorses from the barn?"

I shook my head.

"It's nearly seven o'clock," she cried, clapping her hands. "What are you waiting for? Get going! Zeke! Wake up!"

"I'm up, Kitty," he called.

"Then get down here! Folks'll be arriving in no time."

Kitty hurried about at a furious pace, sweat running from her temples, red hair flying in all directions. She called me and Zeke frequently to run errands and whenever we failed to respond fast enough, snapped, "Boys, they'll be here any minute, get moving!"

Pa spent the morning behind the barn, preparing the barbecue pit and slaughtering one of the old ewes. He moved slowly with the help of a cane.

"You'd think the king of England was coming, for all the fuss she's making," he complained.

Gradually the picnic tables filled with covered bowls and plates as the aroma of roast mutton drifted across the barnyard.

"Too good to waste on strangers," Pa muttered as he surveyed all that Kitty had prepared.

"They're not strangers, Uncle Ray, or at least oughtn't to be."

He grunted.

"I want all three of you in clean clothes when our guests arrive. I'll have none of these filthy overalls."

I was slipping on a fresh shirt when the first carriage pulled up. Pa greeted our guests stiffly, inviting them up to the orchard while I ran out to unhitch the carriage and water the horse. Soon another carriage arrived and then another. For the next hour I ran back and forth from the barn to the house, lining up the carriages along the pasture fence until it looked like a gathering at the county fair. Only the Hejdlings were missing.

Kitty emerged from the house, wearing one of the fresh white blouses and skirts she had purchased on our city trip, her hair neatly pinned. With a slightly feverish flush, she floated among the guests, greeting them, offering glasses of punch, asking after everyone's health and crops. Most of the women came bearing pies and salads. They huddled together near the kitchen, admiring each other's handiwork. The men congregated in the shade of the apple trees, smoking and discussing how close they had come to burning out before the rains arrived. Zeke talked to a few of them about Australian sheep. The youngest children clung to their mothers or sat in a circle around Hunter, petting him and pulling his tail. The older ones studied the roasting sheep awhile, then climbed over the haystacks and tried to flush the kittens from the woodpile. I watched them enviously, keeping to my station beside the barbecue pit, turning the spit and making sure the meat didn't flame up.

When the mutton was ready, Pa sliced it onto a large platter. Kitty announced it was time to eat, and the children came running from every direction, standing impatiently before the picnic tables while their mothers filled their plates. The men knocked their pipes out against their shoes or the heels of their palms, then took a place around the table and waited to be served. The women ate last, some never bothering to sit, complimenting first Kitty and Pa, then each other on the rich feast they had all assembled. Midway through the meal, one of the guests backed his wagon up to the orchard and uncorked a barrel of hard cider. Everyone seemed to laugh more easily after that. Several of the older boys hid under the wagon, drinking directly from the spigot when they thought no one was looking.

As the men loosened up, they began to talk to Pa, offering their condolences about Mama, asking after his leg, our crops, the sheep, our mountain lion, and wondering what kind of farmer I was turning into. "Rumor has it that boy can plow circles around the lot of us," one of them said.

"He's learning," Pa replied cautiously. "My brother-in-law Zeke's been a godsend." It was the first time I'd ever heard Pa praise anyone.

"And your older boy?" another asked.

"Eric's making his way as a painter of pictures," Pa said stiffly.

"I hear he's pretty good," one of the men pursued.

"I'm no judge," Pa admitted. "But they seem to think so down in New York."

When the men got up to stretch their legs, I overheard one of them mention Eric's portrait of Lisa. He seemed happy that "proud Hejdling had been taken down a peg or two."

For all Kitty's good cheer, I caught her glancing over her shoulder whenever a late-arriving carriage pulled up, her face flashing hopefulness then disappointment when it proved not to be Halvard. I was sorry that Bittle had to miss the bonfire.

As the afternoon heated up, I took all the children to the pond for a swim. Several parents followed, some napping in the shade, others rolling up their pants or removing their stockings and dangling their feet in the cool green water. We ran races across the pasture and held a great tug-of-war, the fathers on one side, the mothers and children on the other. As the sun began to turn orange, Kitty called everyone back to the orchard for dessert. The tables were crowded with puddings, cheeses, melons, and pies.

In the gathering twilight, Zeke and I led everyone up to the high pasture, where we had stacked old fence posts, rails, and siding for the bonfire.

We waited until the first star glimmered faintly overhead, then lit the kindling. The fatwood began to crackle and flame, licking the weathered, rotting timbers. Several women fanned the embers with kerchiefs; a few boys crept up close on their bellies and blew into the glowing coals, sending forth showers of sparks like so many fireflies. For a time the fire lay low, sizzling softly, steaming out the moisture in the wood. Then with a roar it burst into flame, soaring high into the air, leaping and dancing, casting eerie, animated shadows on the grass. One boy picked up a stick and threw it into the raging blaze. Another held a long branch to the flames until the tip caught fire, then waved it aloft, painting the darkness with slashes of orange light. Others followed, scouring the pasture for bits of wood. When a flaming stick fell into the grass, starting a small burn, all stick playing stopped.

The fire grew so hot we had to retreat to the shadows. I wondered if Bittle was watching from across the valley. While the adults settled back in the grass, mesmerized by the flames, the children played tag in the dark recesses of the pasture, testing their courage among the trees. Then one by one they drifted back to their parents, laying weary heads upon their mothers' laps.

I was still running with a few of the older boys when I noticed a lone, dark figure approach from the barn. Before the latecomer had come halfway,

Kitty rose and hurried in his direction with the fleetness of a doe. An hour passed and then the guests began to assemble their children and bid Pa good-bye, telling him they'd never enjoyed themselves so much.

"Where's Kitty?" Pa whispered to me, uncomfortable accepting their thanks. "Go find her and tell her to get back here."

I ran to the house, calling her name, but she didn't answer. Her room looked unchanged. Then I noticed her brushes and combs were missing from the top of her bureau. I felt an odd mixture of excitement and grief as I ran back out to help Zeke hitch all the horses.

"She's gone!" I whispered to him.

"With Halvard?"

I nodded.

"Good for her!" he said.

When the last wagon had rumbled down the drive, Pa limped into the house. The kitchen was a shambles: plates and cups everywhere, half-finished pies, empty bowls of fruit, scraps of meat. Hunter, unable to resist the temptation, had pulled down one platter, shattering it on the floor. Outside the cats were leaping from table to table, licking plates clean. Huge colonies of ants swarmed over everything.

"Where's your cousin?" Pa snapped.

"Halvard came for her."

Pa sat down heavily at the kitchen table, then

snorted his surprise. "That boy's got more spine than I gave him credit for." And he smiled.

Mr. Hejdling rode up to the house the next morning in search of his son.

"He was here briefly last night," Pa told him.

"And Miss Kitty?"

"Gone."

Mr. Hejdling's face darkened. "You'll send word the moment you hear from them?"

"Of course," Pa said.

After Mr. Hejdling left, Pa reflected, "I'm the one ought to be upset. He's still got a houseful of help. Look at us—an old cripple, a failed rancher, and a twelve-year-old boy."

"I miss Kitty," I said.

"She'll be back," Pa reassured me.

"What made Halvard change his mind?" I asked.

"He never changed it—he just found his courage, decided it was *his* life, not his father's. I suspect I've got three, maybe four more years before you do the same."

"I'm not going anywhere."

"Things will change. You'll grow tired of all this. World's got much easier ways to make a living. Look at your brother."

A week later we received a letter from Kitty telling us of her wedding and honeymoon. She and

Halvard had taken the steamer to New York and seen Eric. "By the time you read this," she wrote, "he'll be sailing across the Atlantic for Paris, the whole trip paid for by the sale of his notorious portrait of Lisa." When Pa read that he shook his head and said, "Maybe you ought to learn to paint."

Not long after that, Halvard and Kitty returned, dressed in fine new clothes, a gold wedding band glittering on Kitty's left hand.

"Have you been to see your father?" Pa asked Halvard.

"Not yet."

"He's worried about you."

"I wrote him."

"Have you come to stay?"

"If we're welcome," Halvard replied, looking Pa in the eye.

"You're welcome so long as it doesn't cause you grief at home."

"This is my home now," Halvard declared, looking at Kitty.

"You're giving up a lot," Pa cautioned.

"I'm gaining much more," Halvard said, taking Kitty's hand.

Kitty looked at me and said, "You've changed, Nate." Then she threw open her arms and hugged me.

"We've all changed," Pa reflected, taking hold of Kitty's bag. "You most of all, Mrs. Hejdling."

Kitty flushed at the sound of her new name. "It's still just plain Kitty."

"Nothing plain about you," Halvard insisted proudly.

"No, son, there isn't," Pa agreed.

Halvard went to see his father that afternoon, returning just before supper. It would take time, he told us, but he was confident his father would come to accept them. Gregory and Trudy were happy for him.

The next morning he joined Zeke and me in the field, dispelling the sense of isolation that had always hung about the farm.

Pa's leg recovered only partially and then with the fall dampness seemed to worsen. He rarely complained, but whenever he ate without appetite, we knew he was in pain. Kitty often scolded him for straining himself, blaming him for his own suffering. When she did so in Halvard's presence, he lay an understanding hand upon her arm and she grew silent.

Against my will, I came to like Halvard. Marriage had stripped him of his preening ways. He was not like Pa or Zeke, neither taciturn nor overly talkative. He worked hard and seemed to enjoy the labor for its own sake, for the strain upon his muscles, the warmth of the sun on his back, even for the great hunger and thirst it aroused. He ate with relish and slept as soundly as Hunter, waking not with Pa's hollow sense of duty but with a genuine desire to get back to work, intent on making our farm as prosperous as the one he had given up for Kitty.

We saw nothing of the Hejdlings that fall, but after the harvest the two families began to exchange visits, stiffly at first, then with greater frequency and intimacy, especially after Kitty announced she was expecting. Trudy and Gregory came most often, occasionally joined by Sonja. Only Lisa kept away.

As the weather turned cold, Pa swapped rooms with Kitty and Halvard. He said they would soon need more space for themselves and their baby, and he couldn't manage the stairs anymore. Zeke got working on a cradle, and every night I drifted off to sleep listening to the murmur of whispering voices and the shuffle of bare feet across the hall.

The morning little Millie was born, Kitty lay in the big bed, her red hair flowing over the pillows, wrapped in a joy so bright it made the room glow. When I came in, she was humming the lullaby she used to play on the piano. Millie lay fast asleep in the crook of her arm. "Your dear mama was right," Kitty whispered to me. "The oldest trees do bear the sweetest fruit." Then she leaned over and kissed her sleeping daughter.

Paris, to everyone's astonishment, awakened Eric's appreciation of home. With an ocean between us, he suddenly realized how attached he was to the family, writing long, eloquent letters

about his discoveries overseas. Six months after
Kitty's wedding, we received a package the size
of a window pane. It was a formal wedding portrait: Kitty sitting on the parlor sofa dressed in a
long white wedding dress, Halvard standing behind her in a striped morning coat and top hat.
Unnoticed at first were the rest of us, Hunter in-
cluded, reflected in a blue flower vase on the coffee table. He had captured us all with something
that had not appeared in his earlier portraits—a
hint of yearning.

The next four years passed quickly, with great
changes to house and barn and field. Zeke went
off to the new state agriculture college for six
months, and when he returned we enlarged the
barn with the help of Gregory and Bittle and began raising beef cattle. After Kitty had her twins,
we added two new rooms to the house. Then
Halvard and Zeke began clearing the fields
around the old cabin.

About the time Kitty announced she was expecting her fourth child, I started to grow restless.
A dark, unvoiced anger welled up every time
Halvard climbed to the top of the ridge to fell
more trees. I tried to fight it but only grew more
sullen and unhappy, talking to no one, sleeping
late, keeping to myself. Whenever Kitty asked
what was wrong, I barked, "Nothing," and hurried out of the room. Pa alone seemed to
understand.

And then one spring morning, when the world lay most heavily on my shoulders, Pa suggested we walk up to the old cabin. Like Mama, I had gotten into the habit of going up there whenever life in the big house began to feel too overwhelming, watching the circling hawks and incoming storms, trying to understand the anger surrounding my heart. In the midst of Kitty's burgeoning family, I felt a great loneliness.

Using a cane, Pa limped slowly to the top of the ridge with me, pausing frequently, then sat for a long while on the cabin steps, rubbing his outstretched leg just as Eric had pictured him doing long ago. The surrounding woods had been pushed back, the cabin roof repaired. I should have rejoiced in the transformation but felt I was losing something precious.

"Halvard's done quite a job up here," I said bitterly.

"It's yours if you want it," Pa replied.

"What is?" I asked.

"The cabin, the fields. They belong to you, if you want them."

"But I thought Halvard . . . "

"He's been clearing it for you. He knows what it means to you, what it meant to your mama. He and Zeke'll help you restore it, farm it. Kitty's gonna overrun the big house with her next litter. You'll need a place of your own before long, a place to bring a wife one day."

I looked at Pa a long moment and then felt

the tears come, cleansing my troubled heart. His arm encircled my shoulder, then a flutter of wings drew my eyes skyward. There, just above our heads, her wings as white as the freshening sun, hovered Bianca, blessing my future home.